The
Whisper of the Breeze
from
Pine Trees and
Flowing Streams

By
Jishim Nam

Translated by
Kang-nam Oh

 FriesenPress

One Printers Way
Altona, MB R0G 0B0
Canada

www.friesenpress.com

Copyright © 2023 by Jishim Nam
First Edition — 2023

Translated by **Dr. Kang-nam Oh**

ISBN
978-1-03-918945-4 (Hardcover)
978-1-03-918944-7 (Paperback)
978-1-03-918946-1 (eBook)

1. FICTION, LITERARY

Distributed to the trade by The Ingram Book Company

Table of Contents

Translator's Note

In the hearts of the people throughout East Asian countries, there exists a divine being: the Bodhisattva the Compassionate. This divine being is called Gwan-eum or Gwanseeum Bosal in Korea, Guan-yin in China, Kannon in Japan, and Quan-âm in Vietnam. The original Sanskrit name was Avalokiteśvara—"the Lord who looks in every direction"—to respond to the sufferings and trials of people.

Originally, this bodhisattva was believed to be a masculine figure. Since the twelfth century C.E., however, he has been thought of more often as a feminine bodhisattva. Nobody knows for sure what the reasons were for this interesting and significant metamorphosis. At any rate, he/she is now enshrined in almost all the temples in China, Korea, Japan, and Vietnam, and greatly worshipped as a Madonna of gentle compassion.

I appreciate my son Eugene, who made this English translation more readable.

PROLOGUE:

The Ritual of Cremation

Namu Amita-bul,
Namu Amita-bul.

May he return to the Buddha Amitabha,
May he be reborn to the Buddha Amitabha.

May he be liberated from the
suffering body of this world,
And be reborn in the Blissful Land
abided by the Buddha Amitabha.

The coffin is ready. Sacks of charcoal have been heaped
on top. The sobs of the monks and the tears of the ordinary faithful mingle in the air.

The recitation becomes a litany of mourning as a straw
mat is spread over the sacks of charcoal.

May he be reborn in the Blissful Land,
May he be reborn in the Blissful Land.

An apprentice monk sprinkles kerosene over the pyre and places two balls of burning cotton onto it. White smoke begins to curl around the mat like mist.

> Namu Amita-bul,
> Namu Amita-bul.

The smoke rises from the coffin and drifts into the valley before disappearing into the void, the infinite void.

> Burn evil passions and delusions;
> Burn the dark cloud of ignorance,
> To ascend as a beam of pure light.
>
> Death is an eternal separation;
> The eternal separation wherein
> There will be no meeting, not for a moment.
>
> Life is continuing reincarnations:
> If there is no memory of meeting
> in the previous life,
> How is it possible to recognize
> A meeting in the afterlife?
> Though some say life and death
> are one and the same,
> It remains an indecipherable mystery.
> To suffer the loss of a beloved
> Still remains a heartbreak to me.

Monk Hyegang stands like a sculpture, motionless and without breath. Only his sacred robe flutters slightly in the breeze.

Singleness of mind—if this describes a man's total concentration of consciousness, can it also describe Monk Hyegang's grief?

Blossoming azaleas decorate the surrounding hills, shimmering in the setting sun. Everything is as if from a distance: the shining petals, the trickling streams, the sound of the wooden bells that accompany the chanting. They seem still to fade further and further away. My body feels like a grain floating in a sea of eternity.

> If life is suffering,
> Is it because it exists in the body?
> If all sensations and emotions
> And passions and delusions
> Come from the body,
> Can it be that when the body perishes,
> So does the suffering?
> If the body, now lifeless,
> Should suffer that long
> In a rising flame
> Only to perish,
> Would it not be better if it were not born
> In the first place?
>
> May he be free from rebirth.
> Death is suffering.
> May he be free from death.
> Birth is suffering.
>
> Human existence,
> Isn't it a pity in itself?

*   *   *

"You are the chosen people. To be chosen is to be blessed. But remember also that this blessing came at the expense of thousands of less fortunate people. You must not be arrogant or narrow-minded.

"Also remember that your duty is to attend to the less fortunate, to serve them as light and salt. You all know this passage from the Bible: 'Except a kernel of wheat fall into the ground and die, it abideth alone. But if it die, it bringeth forth much fruit.' This means self-sacrifice. We should be a kernel of wheat that falls into the ground and dies so as to bring forth much fruit. This alone is the true meaning of life."

A scarlet tassel hanging from her ceremonial cap, the university president continued with her speech at the orientation ceremony. Her voice resonated.

In E. Woman's University, the most elegant and magnificent of all institutions, fortunate and blessed faces filled the hall. Parents smiled with content as they gazed on their daughters, as if watching buds come to bloom on a Queen Elizabeth shrub.

I bit my lip and turned away, feeling the pain I had endured so many times since I was small girl. I yearned to leave the pain behind. But it had carved out a place in my heart and now tormented me with no sign of abating.

After the ceremony, I left the hall with the mass of people and, crossing a small bridge, exited through the main gate of the campus. A cold wind sweeping at my throat, I removed the scarf from my coat pocket.

Monk Hyegang had been waiting outside the gate and now came toward me. "I was worried I wouldn't be able to find you among all these people," he said. "Isn't your aunt here?"

Seeing his soft smile, I felt myself go foolish, a tightness at my throat. Loneliness penetrated to the bone like a late autumn wind. I had set my teeth against it from my childhood.

Monk Hyegang said I looked cold. "Let's go somewhere and have a cup of tea." He put his arm gently around my back.

We entered a teahouse. The name of it, Magnon, was carved into a black-scorched length of wood placed above the entrance. Inside, baskets of dried flowers hung around the dim room, making it look vaguely classical. The soothing music of Violetta's operatic aria "Oh, Was That You?" flowed from hidden speakers.

Once we'd sat down, Monk Hyegang smiled, as if determined to cheer me from my sorrow. "The first time I saw you, Jaun, you were a little girl in grade six. Now you're a university student!"

I smiled in return. "You were only a boy then, too—in grade ten."

"That's true. But I remember going to your home in Samcheong-dong, seeing you running around in your pretty green dress."

"So you remember that green dress? You certainly have an eye for color," I said, adding, "Oh, but you were an artist, weren't you?"

"It's still true. If I hadn't painted, I doubt I would have survived those times."

"Then why didn't you pursue it?"

"That's my own personal secret. But you'll know someday, and when you do, you'll also understand why I attend medical school in a monk's robe."

"I still remember how my mother admired that painting you did with all the green stars against the black night sky. Stars are ordinarily painted yellow, but you made them green—all through the heavens."

"So, you remember that picture? Just like I remember your green dress!"

We laughed. Memories of my mother lifted our spirits, even if for a while.

Then, a little haltingly, Monk Hyegang said, "I've brought you a gift from Master Dasol. I hope you will treasure it. He said it was to commemorate your starting university." He placed a purple cloth pouch on the table. Inside it was a rosary made of brilliant amber beads.

I was stunned. "Master Dasol? The professor at the Buddhist university? I've read his articles in newspapers and magazines."

"Yes, that's him."

"But—how does he know me? Why would he send me a gift like this?"

"He has known you for a long time—through me."

This was a puzzle. Why would a great monk send me a gift for entering university? And why would Monk Hyegang have told him about me? He seemed reluctant to explain, so I said nothing and put the pouch into my pocket. The beads have remained there since that day, not as a rosary but as a sort of talisman. It is a reminder of the time I became aware of Master Dasol as a person close to me.

The next Saturday was windy. Dark clouds turned into cold rain. It was too miserable to be springtime. I was on my way to Chogye-sa Temple, having read in the newspaper that Master Dasol was delivering a lecture there.

Entering the lecture hall, I heard the chairman saying, "Now, bow to the master." The lecture was over. I would find out later that because of another temple service, the young people's lecture had been pushed up by an hour.

Though sorry to have missed Master Dasol's talk, I was excited at the prospect of meeting him in person.

Master Dasol was in his seat, eyes closed, hands clasped, looking as enigmatic as a graven image. His features sent a thrill running through me. After some time of deep concentration, he rose.

I went ahead as he moved out of the hall and waited, watching him make his way through the crowd of students. I approached, saying, "Excuse me, but…" Unable to think of what to say next, I shuffled awkwardly.

He peered at me, and suddenly, I felt dizzy. His eyes shone as though from an infinite abyss, so piercing and bright; I could not bear to look into them. I stood lost and embarrassed until he said softly, "You have something you want to say to me? Shall we go somewhere and talk?" He walked toward a teahouse named the Bodhi Tree.

Sitting across from him, my heart pounding uncontrollably, I slid my hand into my pocket and touched the beads of the rosary. Master Dasol was holding his palms together in a meditative pose, as in the lecture hall. After a moment, he looked up.

"You have no hardships?"

"No."

"It must have all been very difficult for you," he said quietly. "But I am grateful that you have so much patience and wisdom." His voice told me he knew that I had lived alone for a long time and that he knew those years had been full of pain. My eyes stung with tears. I lifted my cup of tea and lowered my gaze.

"I hear you've chosen to major in English language and literature in university. I know you will work hard in your field, but I would like to suggest that you also consider studying Buddhist truth, if that happens to be the law of causation for you."

So he knew me. He knew from the moment I approached him at the temple. No—he had known me from long before. What was behind all of this? I ached with curiosity, but kept myself from asking, just as I had not asked Monk Hyegang a few days earlier.

Master Dasol closed his eyes and reflected. "I regret that I could not be of any help to you, Jaun. But properly speaking, one can only help oneself, and no person can truly help another. Whether through studying or training, we must cultivate the discipline of self-help. Now you have passed the most difficult part. I trust you will continue wisely as you have until now."

His words sounded faintly like a final invocation. As I watched him, emotion washed over me like a beautiful sunset.

All the way home, I kept thinking, "Master Dasol has been watching me! For how long, and for what reason! I know he has been close for a long time. Although I couldn't see him, any more than I can see the wind or the heat of the sun, he has always been with me."

That was the only time I met Master Dasol. Fifteen days later, I read in the evening newspaper an obituary announcing he had achieved nirvana.

* * *

The monks and the faithful descend from the mountain, leaving eight monks who will pass the night in vigil. White smoke rises from the funeral pyre and drifts through the valley like clouds. Total silence is everywhere, only the occasional lament of an unseen bird.

A monk uses a bucket to pour water onto the pyre. Once, twice, three times… it dampens the rising flames.

Monk Hyegang comes to me and asks, "Will you stay here, too, Jaun?"

"Yes, I will."

"I'm afraid your clothes are too thin, though there will be a fire during the night."

"I'll be all right. Your clothes aren't any heavier. But…"

"What is it?"

"The other day my aunt gave me a journal my mother had kept. She read in the newspaper that Master Dasol's cremation ceremony would be held today. Then she retrieved this journal from the attic, where I'm sure she'd kept it hidden, and gave it to me."

"A journal written by your mother? Have you read it?"

"No."

"Did your aunt tell you anything about it?"

"She said it was about Master Dasol and my mother. I think she decided to pass it on to me after learning that Monk Dasol had achieved nirvana."

"Your mother probably wrote this when she realized the end was near—like she wanted to leave a record of her life. Now that both of them are gone, maybe we should read it so we'll know what to do with it."

"I think so, too." My mind is shrouded by a fog, but out of the fog emerges a vague idea—the reason why Master Dasol remembered me and was watching me.

The mountain sinks into a deep silence, all its life enclosed in its bosom. The monks have built a fire to keep warm and are now seated around it, talking quietly.

Monk Hyegang and I sit before the fire and unwrap the journal. Out of its cocoon of white tissue, it slowly emerges. Has it been waiting for this very moment?

CHAPTER ONE:
March

With the new school year about to begin, and to supplement what I already knew about my new homeroom class from reading their student profiles, I'd requested that one or two students visit with me in the staff room every day. I hoped to become personally acquainted with each of them—to know their backgrounds as well as their faces.

Reading the profile of one particular student named Hyegang, I was intrigued to find:

> Present Address: Yeongdeung-sa Temple, Jeongreung
> Parent/Guardian: Monk Dasol

I had been a high school teacher for ten years. During this time, I had encountered many students and parents from various backgrounds and situations. But I had never met a student like Hyegang, whose address was a Buddhist temple and whose guardian was a Buddhist monk.

Hyegang was not my student initially but was transferred to my class due to a peculiar incident. The entrance ceremony had been held several days before. As was customary, Hyegang, who had scored highest on the entrance examination, had been asked to read "The Oath of the Entering Class." About that time, the dean of students, who was responsible for arranging the ceremony, stalked into the staff room, his face red with fury.

"We should revoke the admission of that kid. I've heard of some Christian sects refusing to salute the national flag. This kid isn't even Christian, yet he refuses to represent his classmates in the reading of the oath! Ridiculous! This kid says he hates to be called the first in anything. He says he doesn't like to take oaths on behalf of others."

The teachers in the room had a laugh about this. It was beyond common sense. Something like placing first in an exam or taking the oath as a representative of your fellow classmates, this was an honor and a privilege. Now here was a student rejecting what we'd always taken for granted!

We discussed whether Hyegang should be expelled from the school or be allowed to remain. After some debate, we decided that he be allowed to remain, on the condition that the student who had placed second on the exam be recommended to read the oath for him. The general consensus was that Hyegang was too bright a student for the school to lose and that the reason for his refusal was not that he was a bad student at heart, but that he held some idiosyncratic views.

The dean of students, who had been pushing for Hyegang's expulsion, accepted the decision finally but insisted that Hyegang be transferred from his class to another. Under this arrangement, Hyegang became my student, while the student who had placed second was moved from my class to the dean's.

That was how I came to know Hyegang. As time passed, he became a puzzle to me as well.

The staff room, large enough to seat all the teachers of the school, was empty. The teachers had gone for the day, and now there were only the desks and the chairs. I was sitting alone, gazing out of the window, ablaze with the light of the setting sun, when Hyegang entered the room. He was tall; his face, serene.

"Come in. Where have you been?"

"In the fine arts room," he replied.

"You're a member of the fine arts club?"

"Yes, I am."

"I've learned you live in a temple," I said, trying to sound natural.

"Yes."

"Is the temple your home?"

"Yes."

"Then Monk Dasol is your father?"

"No, how can a monk be a father?" He firmly denied my assumption.

"I understand there are some monks who are married and have families. Isn't that true?"

"Yes, but Monk Dasol subscribes to the Chogye sect and he's a professor at a Buddhist university."

"I see I was mistaken. But then, why are you living in a temple?"

"I have no knowledge of the matter." His lips became a thin line.

I stopped with this line of questioning, since it appeared that if I was to continue any longer, it would become painful for him.

"Are you fond of painting?" I asked.

"Yes."

"Western painting?"

"I'm working only in oils right now. But I'd like to do some sculpture in the future."

"Sculpture?"

"Yes, there's something I've always wanted to portray."

"What's that?"

"The Bodhisattva the Compassionate."

"The Bodhisattva the Compassionate?" The answer took me by surprise.

"Yes, I believe the image of the Bodhisattva the Compassionate would crystallize everything I've ever wanted to express."

"I see," I said vaguely. The Bodhisattva was an abstract concept to me, something I could not grasp.

Hyegang sat with his palms together on his lap, his eyes fixed on them. It was as if he were praying, as I saw Buddhists do with their hands clasped. And it looked incredibly beautiful. The word "beautiful" is one generally reserved to describe girls, but at that very moment, he transcended the distinction of the sexes. I thought he looked extremely beautiful.

"Did you begin drawing in junior high school?"

"No, I'm not sure when. It might have been when I was in primary school. When I was in the third grade, there was a monk named Dharma-Cloud at our temple. He liked to paint pictures of the Buddhist deities. I thought it might be fun to draw the Four Guardians of the Universe or the Divine General, with their fierce, wide eyes and awesome, muscular arms. I tried to copy these pictures and practiced quite often."

"I see. Isn't it difficult living in a temple, though? Monk Dasol is a good person, I presume."

"Monk Dasol is the one person I respect more than anybody else. I have nothing to complain about."

"That's good. You may go now, but let's talk together from time to time in the future."

Hyegang bowed to me as a way of saying goodbye. As he left the room, I thought I could see a dark shadow of loneliness on the back of that slim, tall boy.

After arranging my books and files in their proper place on my desk, I left the staff room. The windows had by now turned dark, and the sounds of the students who had been practicing sports in the playground had disappeared, too.

Despite the crisp wind, there was every indication that spring had come.

In cool breezes and blowing winds, spring arrives and then it goes. It comes and goes every year like this, though nobody knows from where it comes and to what place it goes. The same is true of life—it comes and it goes.

Jaun had been waiting at the bus stop, and as I got off the bus, she ran toward me. In her pink dress, hair bouncing, she looked just like a butterfly flitting around in the spring wind.

"Hi, Mom!"

"Hi, Jaun. It's cold. You should have worn something warmer."

"I'm not cold." Jaun smiled brightly and held my arm with both hands. I was late because of the interview with Hyegang, so she must have been waiting quite a while.

"Jaun, you said you needed a pair of shoes. Why don't we go to the shoe store over there?"

"Yes, that would be great. I wanted to walk with you."

"You wanted to walk with me? Why?"

"Just because. It's always nice to walk with you, Mom."

I returned her smile. Nearby was a shoe store that made shoes mainly to export to foreign countries. The smile remained on Jaun's face as she looked through its selection, the store owner personally helping her select the best pair.

"How do you like these, Mom?"

I nodded and said they were very pretty. The owner wrapped the pair of shoes, beige with thick rubber soles, in a bag and handed them to Jaun. He stroked her hair as if praising her prettiness.

Jaun held my arm tightly as we came out of the store.

"Mom, we changed desk mates at school today, and I feel terrible about it!" As if it were really terrible, she released my arm and covered her face with her little hands.

"My new desk mate is sloppy and dirty. Her teeth are gray, and her neck is dark because of the dirt. And there's a blue birthmark around her eye, like a bruise." Jaun traced a circle around her left eye with her finger.

Trying not to laugh, I said, "You're always complaining about your desk mates. I'm afraid you'll complain about your life mate later."

"I'm afraid of that, too, Mom." She giggled. I laughed with her.

"You're only in grade six, and you're already worried about marriage?" I asked, widening my eyes.

"Come on, Mom. It's because I'm in grade six. Didn't you think about marriage when you were in grade six?"

"I didn't think about it even when I was in grade twelve."

"Oh, Mom, you must be joking. Did you know Dad long before you got married to him?"

"No."

"You mean your marriage was arranged? You met Dad through someone else?"

"Yes."

"Did you love Dad?"

"Yes, I did."

"Was he nice and handsome?"

"Yes, he was."

"I don't know why he died so young. All the other kids have fathers, except me."

Suddenly the smile had disappeared from Jaun's face, and it looked like tears were forming in her eyes.

"Jaun, Dad wanted to stay with you longer, but that kind of thing can't always be done the way people wish. If you talk about Dad, Mom becomes sad, too. From now on, let's try not to talk about him, okay?"

Jaun looked up at me with a smile and nodded obediently, but her face brightened only slightly. She walked silently, holding tightly onto my arm and resting her head against my shoulder.

"Jaun, I talked with one of my students today and learned that he's excellent at drawing. You're fond of drawing. How would you like it if I invited him over to our place someday?"

"That's a good idea, Mom. I'm always happy to have visitors." She looked at me, her face bright once again.

Loneliness—this loneliness—when did it begin to occupy the tiny heart of this little girl?

We made our way slowly up the hill. Walking along this path always felt like a stroll. We could see the prime minister's residence, and Samcheong Park. In the distance, there were cherry blossoms and acacia flowers, green shrubs all around. Autumn would bring color to the leaves. The top of this small hill was where we watched the passing of time.

"Mom, what's his name?"

"Hyegang. Hyegang Chung."

"What a strange name."

"Not to me, not exactly."

"Is he good at his studies, too?"

"Certainly. He achieved the highest score in the last entrance exam."

"How great!" Jaun sounded excited. "Mom, be sure to invite him over."

"I'll be sure to do that." I smiled at Jaun as I rang the doorbell.

This was a daily routine. Except for on those days I phoned home saying I would be late, Jaun always waited for me at the bus stop. Then we would walk up the hill together, talking.

Our housemaid Dougienei, whom we called Auntie, opened the door.

"You've come?" she said in greeting. "You're a little late today."

Dougienei spent the whole the day by herself, so each time Jaun and I returned home, it was a highlight for her, one that raised her spirits very much. Our home was like that: a girl and two women with lonesome hearts, each lonely in her own way, living together but hiding their true faces as much as they could.

After talking a little with Dougienei, I went upstairs to change out of my clothes.

This two-story house had been home for my husband and me. Upstairs, there were two bedrooms, a bathroom, and a long hallway, wide windows on both sides of it. Jaun and I used the upper floor, while Dougienei lived down-stairs, taking care of the household and of us. The hallway was lined with books. I'd gotten rid of many of the medical books my husband had used, but the books that remained were among the things I valued most in our house. I was grateful for so many books I could enjoy reading.

My late husband had been an enthusiastic book collector. He liked to buy as many books as he could, even those not related to his field of study. Almost every day, he brought home a book or two on topics of general interest. He was a gynecologist and a dedicated professional. He maintained deep affection for his family and made it his responsibility to take care of them. He was a knight in many ways, one who had prepared a four-horse carriage to take his family on a long journey. But against his best intentions, and despite all the affection and sense of responsibility that stood behind them, he left Jaun and me to go on his own journey.

At supper, Jaun said, "Mom, this kimchi is delicious. Try some." She picked up the bowl of kimchi and placed it in front of me. The kimchi was made of fresh radish leaves.

"Thank you." I smiled at how she had become so considerate. At four, she lost her father; now at twelve, she was taking care of her mother. "Did you have a good day at school?"

"Yes, Mom. But there was something embarrassing during music period."

"How could that be? You sing very nicely and play the piano quite well. How can you be embarrassed in music period?"

"The whole class was singing 'The Milky Way,' but they were singing so low that I started singing an octave higher. The teacher and the other kids all laughed. I still blush when I think about it."

"Really?" I said. "I had a similar experience once."

"You did? When?"

"It was a long time ago. When I was taking the entrance exam for junior high school, one examiner asked me to sing 'Autumn Wind.' I was about halfway through the song, when I forgot the melody. I'm embarrassed even now when I think of that time."

Jaun laughed. "You did something like that? We have something in common! I am just like you."

"You should be better than your mother."

"I like you best. I want to be just like you." Jaun leaned over and kissed me on the forehead. After dinner, we peeled a tangerine and shared it.

"Jaun, I'd like to rest for a while. Could you study in your room by yourself?"

"Sure, Mom. But why do you get so tired these days?"

"Maybe because it's spring."

A worried look crossed Jaun's face as she followed me up to my room. Once I was in bed, she pulled the blanket snug around my shoulders.

I fell asleep to the faint sounds of Dougienei washing the dishes. Sleep pulled at me into a bottomless abyss, as if I were a heavy stone.

After signing my name in the attendance book in the staff room, I dropped in on my class to see how they were doing in morning study period. As I made my way back to the staff room, a black limousine pulled up to the front of the school, and out of its rear door emerged the music teacher, wearing a jade green one-piece dress. She waddled toward the staff room, her large breasts preceding her, while the chauffeur, in black tie, bowed at her backside.

This was a regular morning scene, but it made me laugh every time. When I entered the staff room, the music teacher was clutching her compact, putting the finishing touches on her makeup. "I like your blouse, Mrs. Kang," she said in her high voice when she saw me. "I bet it's silk."

"No, it's just nylon. You can wash it in water."

"My goodness! It looks like silk, though."

"Since you're always wearing silk, everything must look like silk to you."

"That might be true," she said. "By the way, are you going to see *Aida* tonight?"

"I believe operas are a music teacher's domain. I can never understand them."

"You may be right, especially since tonight's opera company is from Germany." Chuckling proudly, she deposited the compact into her purse and retrieved an exquisite pearl necklace. She raised her plump arms to put it around her neck.

"If only she would chew some gum or something," the fine arts teacher whispered beside me. "I suffer from indigestion every morning when I see her. I can't stand it. It's really disgusting."

I smiled at him as I took out the daybook that listed the extracurricular activities for my class. At the beginning of each school year, I planned specific activities for each month of the year ahead. This was something I took care to do, so as not to waste time later.

Chapter One: March

The school attendant rang the bell for the teachers' morning meeting as the principal marched into the staff room, notes in hand, and the teachers waited patiently in their seats. This was an everyday routine that never offered anything new or informative. At each of these meetings, the principal would read long, lifeless theories on education, probably quoting from newspapers and old textbooks.

On the Monday before, there had been a general meeting in the playground with all of the teachers and students. As the principal droned on with his talk, the geography teacher came over to where I stood and whispered, "It's said that a teacher makes his profession by using only the mouth, but even for this, you need at least some sense of how to use it. Look at the principal! In everyday life, he resorts to all kinds of Machiavellian trickeries, but in front of the students, he suddenly becomes this moralistic sage. Isn't it too much?"

"It's the same with us, too," I responded, rather coldly.

"Now you're sounding like a moralistic sage, too."

"Don't embarrass me."

"You're right. We're all in the same boat," he said in a self-mocking voice and returned to his place.

Everybody is better at saying things than doing them. Maybe this discordance between what we say and what we do is why so much importance is given to living up to our words. The geography teacher pointed out that we, as teachers, make our livings with our mouths. The profession disappoints me. I listen to things that I know are empty, and I say things that I know are empty.

After the morning meeting, I went to my classroom with my attendance book, a teacher's notebook, and a small card of famous quotations. It was a practice of mine to begin each day of classes with a selection from *The Tolstoy Diary*. The book had been influential to me when I was young, and divided into three hundred and sixty-five parts, one for each day of the year, it seemed appropriate to use for this purpose. On its pages were not only Tolstoy's own writings, but also words written by history's greatest thinkers, both Eastern and Western, past and present. By reading from this book to my students, I hoped to provide them with the opportunity to learn from the wisdom and insight of these great sages.

The practice seemed to have been effective. Graduates of my class told me of the impact that these ideas from Tolstoy's book, which they listened to every morning, had on their individual lives. And I couldn't be certain if this was the reason, but there had not been one single incident of violence in my classes, which is unusual for a boys' high school.

I finished this morning's session by reading a passage from Victor Hugo's *Les Miserable*, as quoted in *The Tolstoy Diary*. Leaving the room afterwards, my eyes happened to meet with Hyegang's. His face was flushed, and his gaze sparkled. I smiled at him with my eyes.

While I was taking a break after the day's third session, Mrs. Hahn came to me. "Our Daddy, I mean my husband is going out into the field today to do some work, so I need to get home early. If anybody notices my absence at the teachers' afternoon meeting, could you say I've gone to see the parents of a student?"

"Is he leaving tonight?"

"Yes, with his students."

"I see."

"The results of this study will be broadcast on television. I'll let you know when the time is set, Mrs. Kang."

"Thank you."

"I would love to move back to the United States, but Daddy, I mean my husband insists on devoting himself to exploring the historic relics of this country. When he's reading a book, sometimes, he smacks his lips, as if he was eating something delicious." She chuckled.

"That's a true scholar."

"I'm sure Jaun is class representative of her class. My daughter, Sookyung, is class rep this year, too. Her teacher tells me she could not wish for a better student for the job than Sookyung."

"She must be smart, like her mother," I replied vacantly, wishing she would leave soon. Even short chats with this woman tired me, or gave me a headache.

"I hear the music teacher makes 4.6 million Won a month just in the interest on her money. It sounds like a fairy tale. But they say her husband is pathetic. He has no profession but insists that his wife teach at the school. Maybe he thinks that being a high school teacher is a mark of prestige."

"Don't be so critical. We're all in the same boat."

Mrs. Hahn had come to me only because she wanted to gossip about the music teacher. It was amusing to think that the pearl necklace the music teacher had put on this morning might have irritated Mrs. Hahn.

Mrs. Hahn is the wife of a professor at Y. University. By circumstance, she appears upper-class and cultured, but now and then she reveals herself to be completely helpless in the presence of power, insatiably greedy before wealth. I know people with ugly faces who partner in the crime of bothering each other. Still, it saddens me to think that one's personal development can be so stunted, that one might become nothing more than like Mrs. Hahn. All I find around me is illusion, and illusion only.

The music teacher with an endless well spring of money, the English teacher whose pride rests on being a scholar's wife, the principal who preaches the principles of education every morning, and I, a supposed teacher of students—we are hopeless. We are empty shells. We can be crushed without a sound. The life of light, not of shadows—will I never find it?

I remember what Faust once said:

> I've studied now Philosophy
> And Jurisprudence, Medicine,
> And even, alas! Theology
> All through and through with ardor keen!
> Here now I stand, poor fool, and see
> I'm just as wise as formerly,
> Am called a Master, even Doctor, too,

Chapter One: March

> And now I've nearly ten years through
> Pulled my students by their noses to and fro
> And up and down, across, about,
> And see there's nothing we can know!

Faust laments to find he cannot understand anything, despite his learning. And disappointed by the limits of man's wisdom, he sets out on a journey of the spirit, on a quest to experience the limitless universe in that way. How can I expect to see the mystery of life that was closed even to Faust? My wisdom is no bigger than the tip of a hair.

For extracurricular activities period, I led the literature club out to the schoolyard. After asking the students to compose a short story titled "Early Spring," I sat beside the flower bed and watched the red peony buds that were now pushing out of the ground. They looked like the tips of writing brushes. Each year, the sight of peony buds was a sign for me that spring had finally come.

There was a flower garden beside the countryside house I'd grown up in. It was decorated with pretty rocks, and around its edges were glass bottles pushed upside down into the ground. Glass bottles were hard to get during those times, so this flower garden was a luxury in the village.

Of all the flowers that were planted in that garden, red peony buds were the first to come up each spring. I will always remember the dynamic power of life I felt when I looked at those buds.

The students handed in their scrawled manuscripts to me while I checked their names one by one. I gathered these manuscripts and returned to the staff room.

As the school's teacher of Korean language and literature, I was charged each year with supervising the literature club and its creative writing activities. But I always felt uneasy with the job because I myself did not write very much.

The fine arts teacher looked up as I entered the staff room. "Mrs. Kang," he said. "That Hyegang is really strange, don't you think?"

"He's a little different."

"Yes, he's quite a fellow." The fine arts teacher laughed. "Every day, he comes to the art room and draws most diligently. But whenever I come near him, his face tightens and he looks at me with those sharp eyes."

"Why?"

"I don't understand it exactly, but he says he wants to express perfect purity, something no one has ever expressed before."

"But why doesn't he let you look?"

"He thinks that if I look at his drawings, this would contaminate them and spoil their purity."

"How interesting. Perfect purity—something no one has ever expressed before. That sounds wonderful."

"I was right in thinking you were the best teacher for him." He laughed again. "I thought it was good when Hyegang was transferred to your homeroom the other day. You're the only teacher who could accept an eccentric like him."

"You mean I'm eccentric, too, don't you?" I smiled at him.

The fine arts teacher was around five years younger than I was and quite talented as an artist. I could feel comfortable talking with him.

The music teacher began laughing loudly at something, and the fine arts teacher glared at her for some time before whispering to me, "Mrs. Kang, I don't understand why Raskolnikov should have felt guilty for killing that pawnshop owner. The harmful and useless are harmful and useless through and through."

"Why are you thinking about Raskolnikov all of a sudden?"

"I'm thinking thoughts very similar to his right now."

"What?"

"If I had an atelier of my own and enough time, there is no doubt I could produce a masterpiece. My heart bursts with images I want to express, but I lack the environment to bring them out. Now, look at the music teacher. She eats, wears clothes, and sleeps. It doesn't make sense for her to have all this money, just to maintain this hollow body. I look at her each morning, and it's like I'm looking at a lump of maggot-infested flesh.

"What a thing to say."

"It's true. The human body is nothing but a lump of maggots."

"That's awful."

"Several years ago, I watched some people exhume a body to move it to another grave. When they dug the body up, it was decayed and all covered over with white maggots. If you think about it, that's all a human body is, isn't it? Without a spiritual aspect, you're just a lump of white maggots."

I said nothing, so he continued.

"I'm not saying you're like that, Mrs. Kang. I can smell your fragrance. Your body isn't like that."

"Please, that's enough," I said finally.

The fine arts teacher began to say something, but the bell rang, signaling it was time for the teachers' closing session.

All through the meeting, I could not stop thinking about what the fine arts teacher had said. "It's true. The human body is nothing but a lump of maggots." But is it true? Is that all we are? Eat, wear clothes, and sleep... we do these things every day to maintain ourselves, but why, if our bodies are nothing but a dwelling place for ugly worms?

My heart was still quivering as the meeting ended, and I entered the classroom for closing session with the students. I delivered a short talk about nature and the importance of environmental protection, then examined the students' belongings.

"Mrs. Kang, let's sing 'I Dream of Jeanie,'" Changho called out near the end of the session.

"Yes, why don't we," I said. While I began each day by reading a passage from *The Tolstoy Diary*, I ended each day with a song. In principle, only folk songs were allowed, but I thought a pop song on occasion was all right.

I dream of Jeanie with the light brown hair,
Borne like a vapor on the summer air...

Chapter One: March

The boys in their black school uniforms sang with the feeling that must have been beginning to bud inside of them. Their faces looked clear and pure; even the roughest students sang well and with genuine feeling. After the song, I received their bow and left the room.

The sky was gray, and there was a chill in the wind. It was too cold for springtime. According to tradition, cold and windy weather in the spring season meant that nature was jealous of the flowers. But also it seemed true to me that new life brought pangs of birth to nature that delivered it.

The repetition of the daily routine tired me, especially at the beginning of each school year, when there were many trivial jobs to be done. Mrs. Hahn often said, "I envy Daddy, I mean my husband. He gets six-month vacations, and even during the school year, he lectures only six hours a week. We high school teachers are loaded with classes twenty-four hours a week, and, on top of that, there are so many other things to get done. How can anyone expect us to educate our students like this?"

She was bragging about her husband even while she complained. But she had a point: Teaching classes was not the main source of our headaches. It was the paperwork—sorting them, filing them, replying to them. We brought these papers home regularly, just to finish in time. Then there was the responsibility of disciplining the students. Adolescence brought with it many changes, and the hearts of these boys were more unpredictable than the spring weather. Not a day passed without some problem.

It was Saturday and after the fourth session. I was busy tallying up the student attendance for the week when the biology teacher pushed into the staff room, practically dragging Hyegang by the collar. He ordered Hyegang to get down on the cement floor and assume the push-up position, and began striking him on the hip with a long rod. The rod broke in two pieces. I felt my blood boil as I saw what was happening.

"Could you tell me what is the matter?" I walked over to where they were.

"We should send this fellow to the dean of students," he said. I glared at him as he continued, "We're dissecting rabbits in class today, and this fellow categorically refuses to do the work. Not only that, he refuses to watch others doing it."

"I see," I said, trying to maintain my composure. "Please have him see me after you've dealt with him."

I returned to my seat as Hyegang straightened his clothes, a pained expression on his face. The biology teacher said a few more words but canceled his original intention of sending Hyegang to the dean of students. "Go to your homeroom teacher for your instructions," he said, and left the room.

Hyegang stood in front of me, his head low. I felt sadness at seeing his slim body.

"You'd better go and apologize to the biology teacher, and attend the rest of the class. Come see me after the closing session. Do you understand?"

"Yes." Hyegang bowed to me. Once he'd left the room, the teachers who had been in the room began to give their thoughts.

"What does his father do?" asked the physical education teacher.

"He teaches at a university." I didn't want to give details about such things as the Buddhist temple and monks and have the teachers see Hyegang differently.

Hyegang came to me after closing session. As usual, his face was serene.

"Were you planning to draw awhile before leaving for the day?" I asked.

"Yes."

"I'm going home now. Won't you come with me?"

"I'll come." He accepted my invitation readily and went to the fine arts for his school bag while I arranged my desk. I considered going to a small bakery that was nearby to talk but then decided to take him to my home. I remembered the promise I'd made to Jaun, and also it would be good for Hyegang to see what an ordinary home looked like.

"There's a young lady waiting for you." I smiled.

"A young lady?"

"Yes, my little daughter."

"Oh, I see."

We stopped in at a stationery store by the front gate so I could phone home. Jaun answered the phone. "Do you have to work tonight again?" she asked.

"No, I won't be late. I'm bringing someone. Will you ask Aunt Dougienei to prepare supper for an extra person?"

"Yes, but what guest?"

"The student I told you about the other day."

"Hyegang Chung?"

"Yes, that's right."

I smiled at Hyegang. "My daughter remembered even your last name."

There was a group of students from my homeroom class waiting at the bus stop. When they saw us, they came closer. "Mrs. Kang, where are you going with Hyegang?" they bantered. "Can we come, too?"

These students had cheered at the entrance ceremony upon hearing that I was assigned to be their homeroom teacher. Later, when I asked in class why the announcement was something to cheer about, they joked, "That's natural. There's the principle of relativity." I laughed with them.

Now I could not be sure if the principle of relativity applied here or not, but I found it much easier to deal with boys than girls. In a case like this, if they had been girls, they would have turned their backs out of jealousy.

"Mrs. Kang, don't take just Hyegang, take us, too. Five doughnuts for each of us should be good enough." They laughed heartily. We said goodbye to the cheerful boys as we got on the bus.

"Do your relatives invite you to their homes from time to time?"

"No, I don't have any relatives."

"Nobody visits you either?"

"No."

"You never go out then?"

"I stay in the temple most of the time. There's an errand to run for Monk Dasol once a month."

"What's that?"

"He sends me to his brother's home. Nothing really needs to be done, but he wants me to have a meal in an ordinary home."

"He must be very considerate if he's paying attention to matters like that. You're growing very quickly now. The vegetarian diet at the temple might not be enough for a growing boy."

I wondered about the relationship between Monk Dasol and Hyegang. Though I couldn't know its exact nature, it seemed to me that Monk Dasol was carrying out his care-taking duties with deep and tender affection.

"Why did you refuse to participate in the rabbit dissection today?"

"Because I'm not going to be a doctor or a scientist."

"That doesn't mean you should skip the class, does it?"

"I can do anything in the class, but I will never slit the belly of an innocent animal for no reason."

"Maybe there is a reason. It's probably quite difficult to learn about anatomy otherwise."

"It would be necessary for me to learn about anatomy if I was intending to major in medicine or biology. But I'm not interested in those fields."

"No one knows that. Many things of the present are not as controllable as we would like. How can we be certain of the future?"

"I won't dissect animals. My whole body trembled when I saw the rabbit's eyes. It was quivering with fear. How can you put your knife to the heart of a living rabbit?"

I nodded. I could still remember a time in high school when I trembled with fear at seeing the pumping heart of a frog after we'd opened its belly. Afterwards, we buried the frog in a corner of the schoolyard and someone sang a small hymn. It was not a good memory. It was a reminder of a time when we'd taken an innocent life.

Jaun ran to us as we got off the bus.

"Did you wait long, Jaun? Say hello to Hyegang. Hyegang, this is my daughter, Jaun."

"Hi, Hyegang." Jaun bowed her head slightly and held onto my arm. A smile lit Hyegang's face. As we walked up the hill, Jaun's chatter cheered us like a lark in springtime. When Hyegang wasn't looking, Jaun turned to me and pointed at her green dress. "Do you like the dress. Does it look all right?"

"Yes, it looks perfect. Very pretty," I whispered in her ear.

We had arrived home, and Jaun was bubbling about this and that as she walked about the house. She looked thrilled to be hosting a guest in her home. My heart became heavy at seeing Jaun's happy face. She deserved to be like other children, who had fathers and brothers and sisters and who were too young to know loneliness. The least I could do was arrange an enjoyable evening for the two lonely children.

"Hyegang, will you go to Jaun's room and draw a picture for her? I'd like to rest for a while."

"Yes, Hyegang, will you draw a picture for me, please?" Jaun said.

I watched the two go into Jaun's room before I went into my own and lay down on the bed. Fatigue came to me so strongly these days.

Jaun and Hyegang came into my room about an hour later. "Mom, this picture is wonderful, isn't it?" Jaun was holding up a watercolor. It had a black sky and many green stars like jewels. How did he make those green stars so bright?

"Yes, it's excellent," I agreed. "I'll put it in a frame tomorrow and hang it in your room." I looked at the two of them. By the glow on their face, I could tell this was the happiest either of them had been in a very long time.

Lonely children. Tender feelings touch their lonely hearts like the sweet smell of flower petals....

It would be nice if the two children could grow up as brother and sister.

Hyegang stood up, explaining it was time for him to go home. I told him he could get to Jeongreung by transferring buses at Gwanghwamun and said goodbye to him. After he left, Jaun looked up at me with eyes that sparkled. "He is a wonderful boy, isn't he, Mom?"

"Yes. If you like, I'll invite him over from time to time."

"I would like that. Please ask him again, Mom."

I could hear Jaun's clear voice as she sang "A Dotted Bellflower" in her room and also a bustling sound. Probably she was tidying up her room. But soon, she became quiet, likely having fallen asleep, a smile on her face.

CHAPTER TWO:

April

A cool breeze touched the inside of my chest. As Monk Dasol spoke, I could hear the whisper of breeze moving deep in the forest.

"According to Buddhism, who we meet in this world is determined by the law of causation. I believe it was this law that brought Hyegang and me together."

"Hyegang mentioned he has been living at the temple for some time."

"He came to me when he was four and now he is seventeen," Monk Dasol said. "One might say that is a long time."

"How did it happen that he went to you when he was so young?"

"That is why I asked to meet with you today. I wanted to tell you about that. But now I feel hesitant to explain. It is something known only to myself. None of the other monks at the temple know, and certainly not Hyegang himself."

"I see."

"The other day, I found this note among Hyegang's belongings." He handed me a small piece of paper, folded in half.

I opened it. In Hyegang's handwriting, it read:

> When I look at my homeroom teacher, I feel colors, an infinite array of colors. I believe these colors will enable me to express the image I've always longed to express. I have never experienced this before, never before in my life.

I looked at Monk Dasol.

"Obviously, you are very special to him," he said.

I could think of nothing to say.

"Yeongdeung-sa Temple is a place for celibate monks in training. I left my home life thirty years ago. So, in many respects, I feel very unqualified to take care of Hyegang."

"I'm sorry to trouble you," he continued when I said nothing. "But I would appreciate it very much if you would take him into your special consideration."

"I understand."

"For you to know Hyegang better, I think I should tell you how Hyegang came to be under my care in the first place," Monk Dasol said pensively.

"It was thirteen years ago, on a day just like today. There was no class at the university that afternoon, so I was at the temple when a man came with a child. He sent the child to play in the courtyard before he approached me alone. He bowed to me reverently, told me he had been attending my lectures for almost a year. Then he asked me to take his child. At first, I was unprepared to agree to this unexpected request. But then he lifted his face and looked directly at me. The man was a leper, in the early stages of the disease, and not seriously deformed, but it was nevertheless visible at first sight. His expression was one of complete despair. As if sensing my thoughts, he pulled out the child's birth certificate from his pocket and put it on the ground in front of me. He bowed again and left by the back door. And this was how Hyegang lost his father and came under my care."

"I see."

"Although he was young, Hyegang seemed accepting of his fate and adjusted well to the new environment. My affection for him grew as time passed. As you know, he is intelligent and has a talent for drawing. I believe he was born with a clear nature."

"I don't know that much about leprosy. Isn't it hereditary?"

"According to the literature I've read over the years, no definite theories on the cause of the disease have been proven. I know only that Hyegang is perfectly healthy."

"I see."

We were silent for a moment, Hyegang's serene face in my mind. How could that boy, as clear as morning dew, have such a fate?

"Hyegang's father never came back. He may never come back."

"How about other family?"

"Nobody came. Hyegang may as well be a boy fallen from the heavens."

As if trying to ease the impact of all this new information, Monk Dasol smiled at me gently. It helped to relax me a little, and I said half-jokingly, "The other day, one of the teachers asked me what Hyegang's father did for a living, and I replied that he was a professor. I suppose if Hyegang is a child fallen from the heavens, you could be his father."

"Possibly." He laughed.

We smiled together, and for the first time, I felt at ease.

"You were talking about the law of causation."

"It is said that to understand the law of causation is to attain the enlightenment. One might talk about the law of causation on a theoretical level, but complete understanding is possible only with the achievement of Buddhahood."

"I've heard that Buddhism explains the ground of all existence in terms of the Buddha-nature, or Suchness."

"That's correct. All aspects of existence may be seen in the ripples of ignorance moving over the Buddha-nature. Although these ripples do not know why they move, they move with unimagined power. It is this power that guides life as it progresses through the cycle of appearance and disappearance."

"That sounds like my life. I don't know why I live, yet I struggle to keep pace every day."

"That's right," he said. "That's the case with me, too."

Monk Dasol had practiced spiritual training for many years and was a professor of religion at a university: How could he express his spiritual state so humbly? It was refreshing. I'd grown tired of people trying to make small things big, ugly things beautiful.

"Then, how is the law of causation relevant?" I asked.

"As I've said, I don't fully understand it, but as far as the theory is concerned, it goes like this: Let's use the example of water. Water may be found in all places and takes many forms. It is in the sea, in rivers, streams, springs. When it is heated, it evaporates to become mist. When it is cooled, it condenses to become rain, hail, snow, or ice. But despite all these different forms, water's fundamental nature remains the same. There is waterness itself. The same is true of us. The law of causation states that although we may take various forms, the ground of these forms remains the same. This ground is what is called Suchness."

"So, if we transcend these differences in form and return to that Suchness, that is how we attain the Buddhahood?"

"Yes. But in order to return to the original nature of our being, we must train ourselves and purify our minds."

"It seems we should have remained Suchness itself in the first place. How did we lose ourselves in these ripples of ignorance?"

"Well…" Monk Dasol smiled. "I don't know the answer myself. Perhaps when you reach the tenth stage of the bodhisattva, you may answer that question for me."

I did not ask any more questions because the questions I had could not be fully answered by theory alone, and because theoretical explanations could not be fully understood.

Monk Dasol did not try to show off his knowledge and insights, nor did he try to impose his beliefs.
An hour spent with him was enjoyable. How could I
describe it? Satiation—as when a long gnawing hunger is
finally satisfied.

In front of the Bodhi Tree teahouse, Monk Dasol said
he would entrust Hyegang to my special care, and we
parted. I watched the gray sacred robe fade into the darkness, and once again, I heard the whisper of wind moving
deep in the forest.

Dougienei opened the door when I returned home. With
a sullen look, she said, "You're late. Come in."

Behind her, Jaun called out, "Mom, look who's
here? Doug."

"Doug? Is he here on vacation?" I asked Dougienei.

"No, for good," she replied glumly.

"So, he's discharged from the army? Why do you look
so upset then?"

"He and I must have been enemies in our former lives,"
she murmured. "Whenever he sees me, he pumps poison
into the air to kill me."

"Your son has come home after years in the service.
Why don't you welcome him more warmly?"

At this, she muttered, "You don't understand. You'll
never understand the mind of this poor woman." She
went inside.

When I entered the porch, Doug bowed to me. He
was in the uniform of a discharged soldier.

"You've completed your military service?"

"Yes."

"Congratulations. How long has it been since you've been home?"

"I haven't been here in a year."

"That long? Oh yes, one year has passed since then, hasn't it?"

"How have you been, Mrs. Kang?"

"I've been as usual."

Jaun, who had been watching our conversation, spoke. "Mom, you haven't had supper yet, have you?"

"No, Jaun. Would you go to the butcher's and buy a kilogram of beef? Let's prepare a roast for Doug."

Jaun took the money I held out and ran off with fluttering steps.

"Roast beef for me? You shouldn't bother, Mrs. Kang."

"It must be nice to come home after such a long time. Go change your clothes and make yourself comfortable."

When Doug had left the room, Dougienei appeared, drying her hands on her apron. "Roast beef for that damn fellow? He doesn't deserve even a bowl of rice." She continued to mutter as she took my lunch box into the kitchen. I watched her wide back, thinking, "Even a bird feeds its babies. Isn't that woman capable of the affection of a tiny bird?"

Forgetting Dougienei's cold stare, I went upstairs. I was very tired, more than just because I'd come late.

I was lying in my bed when Jaun called out that supper was ready, and I went downstairs. The table, which had looked empty before, now looked full with Doug's presence.

"Doug, help yourself to the beef."

"Thank you."

"I hear they feed the soldiers pretty well these days."

"They serve chicken or pork quite often."

"Really?"

"You look thinner, Mrs. Kang."

"I'm getting older."

"Mom, now that Doug is discharged, I think he should get married. Then Auntie would have a daughter-in-law."

"What good's a daughter-in-law? My own son eats me out of house and home. What a parasite a girl who lives off him would be."

I looked at Doug with sympathetic eyes. His face was grim, but he quickly put a spoonful of rice in his mouth. Since I couldn't be sure what else would come out of his mother's mouth if she continued, I cut her off, saying, "Doug's problem now is to get a job, isn't it?"

"Yes."

"What kind of job do you have in mind?"

"I have no education. I would do anything if given the opportunity."

"Oh, he'll loaf for days. How much that will eat at my heart," Dougienei muttered to herself.

"You should stop," I said finally. "We're a small family. Doug is not a burden. And having a grown male at home is safer for us."

Doug's efforts at calming himself were visible. He and his mother would likely have had a big fight if I had not been there. Dougienei would have cursed her son with a flurry of foul language and cried self-pityingly over her fate. As I looked on now, Doug's angry face reminded me of the circumstances under which he had decided to join the military.

Doug was one of the top students of his high school class. A quiet boy by nature, he studied hard, sometimes through the night, in preparation for the university entrance examinations. But whenever he asked for the money necessary for his schooling, he received only abusive language from his mother. His resentment must have deepened with each time this happened.

One morning, as Doug was about to leave for school, he was scolded for a trivial matter. He went into the kitchen and emerged with a kitchen knife, his face a deadly pale. Fortunately, I had not left for work yet and there was no accident, but the incident showed me that even the natural affection existing between mother and child could not be taken for granted. I began to have doubts and frustrations about the nature of human relationships.

One evening a few days after that incident, Doug came to my room.

"Mrs. Kang, I'm very sorry for so many things." He bowed his head.

"Do you really feel sorry?"

"Yes, I do."

"Then, that's all right. Since when you were seven and you and your mother came to live here, we have lived as family. But the ten years have been tiring for me. How can I stand this? You know, I can't bear it."

"I apologize. I realize I have always caused trouble in a house that would otherwise be peaceful."

"I know your mother is much to blame, but also you should treat her with tenderness. I think she could love you."

"Her? Love me? My mother—that woman is incapable of loving anybody," he cried in despair.

"How can that be?"

"It doesn't matter. I'm all right with it now. Filial piety means nothing to me, anyway. What I've come to tell you is that I'm going to quit school and join the army."

"Join the army? You have only three months before you graduate."

"What's the point of graduating if I'm not going to university?"

"How can you know you're not going to university without even having written the entrance exams?"

"I've made my mind not to spend any more of my mother's money."

"You'd better graduate, though."

"No, I won't spend even one more Won of her money."

"I'll take care of the tuition for the remaining quarter. And if you pass the entrance exam, I'll pay for your registration and the first semester. After that, I think you can take a part-time job and pay your way."

"Thank you, but what's important to me right now is to leave my mother as soon as I can." His voice was thick with resolution.

As firm as he was in his decision, there was no way I could sway him otherwise. He left home a few days later.

One day during the following summer, Doug came to the house, dressed in full uniform, to spend his first vacation. When he saw me, he said, "I came home because I wanted to see you and Jaun. The thought of seeing you again made me glad I had a home to return to." He bowed his head as he tried to stop crying.

I put some roast beef in front of Doug. "Have as much as you can; then rest for a few days. I'm sure you'll find a job if you try."

Doug's eyes were brimmed with emotion. I could feel the *han* in his heart, the grief and the bitterness.

Everyone, to be sure, has experienced *han*, but perhaps it is the most painful when it comes from not loving one's own mother. To have true *han* like this is to know suffering. And one who knows suffering can be saved in any circumstance.

After supper, I put several tangerines on the table and went upstairs to my room. Doug may have been telling Jaun stories about the army. From time to time, I could hear her laugh from downstairs. I lay down in my bed. Only a few hours had passed since I had met with Monk Dasol, but it seemed like a dream I'd dreamt a long time ago.

According to Buddhism, who we meet in this world is determined by the law of causation. Could it be true? From when we are born to when we die, our existence is a succession of encounters. Happiness and unhappiness, suffering, sadness; joy and anger; sadness and pleasure—in the final analysis, these are the results of the relationships we have with our fellow human beings, aren't they?

I have come across many faces until now. Some have made me happy. Some have not. But then, those that did not may bring happiness to others, while those that made me happy may not do so for everyone. The same is true of me. I have brought happiness to some people, while, to others, I have caused pain.

If we meet and share our happiness, it may be because the law of causation delivered a positive result. If we bring suffering, it may be because the law brought a negative one. We would like to live our lives with only good people, but life is not like that. Many times, we meet people we don't like, and many times, we meet people who don't like us. Relationships like these do not result from conscious choices; they're a consequence of reality. I wonder if these consequences of reality are also the result of the law of causation.

Monk Dasol believed the law of causation brought him and Hyegang together. This would assume that all people in this world are interrelated and interdependent. But this poses a dilemma: If we believe that the law of causation operates according to the providence of a supreme being, we are left with so many unsolvable contradictions. If we believe that the law of causation is a law of retribution, this, too, leads to many unanswerable questions. Is it possible, as Monk Dasol says it is, to achieve full understanding through Buddhahood?

I woke up the next day to a bright, clear morning and a light heart.

Doug was already up and about in the yard when I stepped outside on my way to work. He had been pruning the lilac bush and, upon seeing me, gave me a quick smile.

"Why didn't you sleep some more? You deserve to after the hard time you've had."

"I slept enough."

"Well, then have a restful day at home."

"Thank you. You have a good day, too." He followed me to the gate and watched me walk down the road. He was wearing white cotton gloves and holding a pair of pruning shears. I imagined his face to have an expression of loneliness on it, just like with the other members of our little home. I was surrounded by loneliness. Was it because I was a lonely woman? Hyegang, Jaun, Doug—each came to me for support and consolation. But what had I to give?

When I arrived at the school, the fine arts teacher said he was glad I had come early. "We're taking the students to East Nine Tomb Park next Wednesday. There's a sketching contest."

"So?"

"There's going to be a composition contest, too."

"With the sketching contest?"

"Yes."

"Will that work?"

"I'm not sure, but the decision has been made that way."

"Well, I suppose it's been determined then."

"So, as the fine arts teacher and the Korean language teacher, we're supposed to come up with an itinerary for the day and a list of awards."

"Fine."

The music teacher turned toward us and, in her high voice, said, "You'll have a nice time of it."

"A nice time?" the fine arts teacher said. "Why don't you take charge of it then?"

"A sketching and composition contest? I could if it were a music festival. But there's no such thing at our school."

"You should organize an opera. With the money you have, you could prepare a splendid stage, a magnificent one."

"An opera?" The music teacher laughed loudly. "That's a fantastic idea! I wish I could do something like that. I'm so bored as it is. At home, I have nothing to do. At school, too." She continued to laugh heartily as she left the room. She didn't seem to mind that the other teachers were glaring at her.

"That's enough," I said to the fine arts teacher. "It's a sin to harass a person so early in the morning."

"It could never be a sin to harass the music teacher. Never."

"The music teacher is no exception. If you dislike her only because she's rich, then it's cowardice on your part."

"I doubt I could irritate her even if I tried very hard. There are some people who just won't be affected. That's why it could never be a sin to harass the music teacher."

"You're being unpleasant," I said.

"I didn't start it. If she hadn't poked her nose in, in the first place, I wouldn't have talked to her. Why would I?"

"That's enough. This isn't gentlemanly."

"Not gentlemanly? Now, tell me honestly. Didn't it irritate you when she said a few minutes ago that she ought to arrange an opera?"

"She majored in voice. She could do that."

"Even cows would laugh at what she could arrange. A woman who has not the slightest concept of what art is—how could she direct an opera?"

"You sound like a famous artist already."

"Who knows? I could be famous in the future. Anyway, I'm not talking about a person's reputation as an artist. I'm talking about a mind that understands art. How can a person who has never suffered know what art is? The music teacher asked the board of directors that she be allowed to teach only eight hours a week. So she could spare her voice, she said. I don't know where she got this idea of sparing her voice. It's crazy. What does she do with her spared voice, anyway? She knows nothing about life, but still I doubt she's going to ask that her money be spent on preserving her voice when she dies."

"Don't concern yourself about her. Just mind your own path to becoming a great artist."

"I will. I'm going to be a great artist. I hate seeing the world going to pot. I'll be an artist who can take firm hold of the world." The fine arts teacher's mouth shut tight, and I could hear grinding teeth. For some reason, he seemed predisposed to being angered by the music teacher.

The music teacher enjoyed special privileges at the school, because according to rumor, she had donated a considerable sum of money for the expansion of the school. Although the customary teaching load was twenty-four hours a week, she taught eight hours and was not responsible for a homeroom.

With only one class a day to teach, she idled most her time in the staff room. No one there was friendly to her, but she appeared unfazed. To her, it seemed, the only real things in life consisted of eating, wearing clothes, and sleeping. She came with a built-in mechanism that made things easy and convenient for her.

After submitting my suggestions for the composition contest, I went to my class for opening session, my mind preoccupied with the vision of Hyegang's face. Since meeting with Monk Dasol, there had been a struggle between seeing him as a leper's son and the rational understanding that I had to rid myself of those thoughts.

More than ever before, Hyegang's face caught my gaze as I entered the classroom. He had the same serenity about him as always, but this time, a momentary hallucination, one beyond my understanding, took hold. In Hyegang's face, I could see Monk Dasol looking back at me. The strong, piercing eyes, eyes with the power and intensity of fire.

I blinked, and the illusion disappeared, but in my heart, I heard the whisper of a breeze blowing softly from deep within the forest onto Monk Dasol's sacred robe. The cool breeze touched against the inside of my chest, as it had done at my meeting with Monk Dasol.

When I looked at Hyegang again, he was looking back at me, his face a little flushed. Any apprehensions I may have had about Hyegang disappeared, and affection surged in my heart. One thought raced through my head: "I will help him. I will help him."

I left the class after finishing opening sessions, and as I went down the stairs toward the staff room, I gave thanks for the victory I'd accomplished that morning. But what was the power that had enabled me to win the struggle in me?

Classes had ended for the day, and I was sitting in the staff room when Hyegang entered. "Did you meet Monk Dasol yesterday?"

"Yes."

"He's a good person, isn't he?"

"I believe he is."

"I knew you would like each other if you met."

"Like each other?"

"Because you're both good people."

"How do you mean?"

"It's difficult to explain, but you seem to have a certain power in common."

"A certain power?" I thought. That was it! The power that had helped me had come from seeing Monk Dasol's face in Hyegang's and hearing the whisper of a breeze. I felt a certain fear when I recognized this—fear as when sunlight penetrates a cave for the first time and awakens the soul that had been lying dormant within.

With the clock showing five o'clock, the teachers were leaving to go home for the night. I was arranging my desk to leave when Mrs. Hahn, the English teacher, came to me with a smile on her face.

"Mrs. Kang, do you have plans for this evening?"

"Not really, why?"

"If you're not busy, would you care to go to an exhibition with me?"

"An exhibition?"

"Yes, a friend of mine is holding an exhibition at a gallery in Insa-dong, and she has asked me to come."

"An exhibition of Western paintings?"

"No, one for dyed art."

"It sounds interesting."

"Applied arts was her major. She went to the United States to study dyeing when I was there. We've been very close friends ever since."

"I see. I'm not familiar with dyeing at all, but I'll be glad to go with you."

"Thank you. I was afraid you might refuse. And how could I go by myself?" Mrs. Hahn said. She had a way of speaking in a very hushed tone.

I left the staff room with Mrs. Hahn. Some students were practicing somersaults in the schoolyard. "Good night, teachers."

Mrs. Hahn gestured a wave and smiled. She was a short woman with a lean face. There was always an air of culture about her, but it was like a dry flower with no fragrance.

"Mrs. Kang, school life is awfully monotonous, isn't it?" she asked.

"Well, it's become so routine, I have no particular feelings about it."

"The level the students are at has become so low, I'm not even interested in teaching them anymore."

"Maybe English is a difficult subject."

"Their comprehension skills are down to zero. It's practically hopeless."

"You learned English in the United States. Your pronunciation must be very different from what they're used to hearing."

"You may be right. That's why I'm worried that my daughter is going to junior high school here. When I imagine her learning that terrible pronunciation from her teachers, I'm horrified. I'd like to see if I can send her to a junior high school in the United States."

I couldn't believe what I was hearing. How could she send her child to a foreign country? What values and beliefs would the child develop? Would she understand what was truly precious in life? What could this woman possibly be expecting of her child?

"My sister is successful," she said.

"I hear she was always wealthy."

"I don't mean in that sense. Her son has been admitted to the engineering program at S. University."

"I see."

"She bought a car for her son to use and hired a tutor when he was in grade twelve. Her son's extra lessons cost more than six hundred thousand Won a month."

"Is that right?"

"He has been accepted to S. University. That's how I mean she is successful. Many students who are supported like that fail."

"I see."

"My sister does her best in everything, and I envy her. The upstairs floor of her house is incredibly luxurious—a carpet worth seven million Won, and a grand piano."

"You have a carpet and piano, too, don't you?"

"There's no comparison."

"You're well off, too. You own two houses in Seoul. That could be considered rich."

"Those places cannot even be called houses. My sister's house has a landscaped yard covering thousands of square feet."

I was getting tired of responding, so I stayed silent. Thousands of square feet right in the core of Seoul—a person could not step foot on most of it in a whole day. Meanwhile, many people lack even a small area for their families to rest their heads on. How can a person enjoy such tremendous wealth and be comfortable about it? She may think she made her fortune by her own effort, but that ignores the losses of countless people who were not as strong or lucky as she. It would be unforgivable for her not to feel the despair of these people and have pity for them.

I felt a pang at my heart. That I was in the company of Mrs. Hahn made me uncomfortable, as if my clothes were too tight.

"My husband is extremely busy these days putting the final touches on his dissertation," she continued. "He has no time to play with Sookyung. But I think he's receiving his degree at the next convocation."

"That's nice."

"I hear your husband had a doctorate degree."

"Yes."

"That's too bad."

I couldn't be sure whether she felt bad about my husband's death or about the fact that his degree had been wasted. Her continuous talking exhausted me, and the hushed tone of her voice making it even worse. Her cultured nature was constantly on the forefront of her consciousness. The hypocrisy of it all seemed obscene to me.

We arrived in Insa-dong, with all its antique shops. When we'd reached the gallery, Mrs. Hahn pushed me ahead, her hand on my back. "Here we are, Mrs. Kang."

The entrance of the exhibition hall was crowded with potted plants and flower baskets. As if it was their singular purpose to advertise who had given them, each of them wore a red ribbon, the name of the giver written on it in brush.

Displays hung on the walls inside the exhibition hall, and in the middle of the room, there stood a middle-aged woman in a cherry-blossom-pink evening gown. On seeing Mrs. Hahn, the woman gave a wide smile that matched the flowers outside and came to shake hands with her. I watched with weak humor as they exchanged exaggerated expressions of friendship.

I was aware that the field of dyeing was not a pure art, but still it seemed inappropriate to me that most of the displays there were hung with the intention of selling them. I wondered how these items of commerce could be shown in a gallery under the guise of an art exhibition.

The two women, sometimes speaking in English, did their best to communicate warm feelings to each other, but it was apparent they were not close friends. There was a competitive edge to their conversation, and jealousy coiled around their words like serpents around their hearts.

The woman greeted each of the visitors with the refined smile of a coffee shop hostess. Ostensibly, it was to show her gratitude to these people who had come to appreciate her work, but the delivery was artificial and shallow. When Mrs. Hahn turned to me, wanting to introduce me to her friend, I said, "I need to get home. Why don't you stay as long as you like?" I left the hall.

It would have been courteous to smile, praise the work, and buy a piece before leaving, if only to save face for Mrs. Hahn, but I was sure I couldn't do it. I lacked the ability to disguise my feelings. If the art on display had been for sale like items at a street market, I might have bought one as I might have bought a scarf, without struggle. When I got out into the street, I felt empty inside.

Despair over human nature flooded through me, as I wandered through Insa-dong and into Anguk-dong. The entrance of Chogye-sa Temple came into sight. There were many stores selling Buddhist articles in front of it, and I stopped at one, browsing absentmindedly. I could hear the recitation of the *Thousand Hands Sutra* flowing out through an open window:

May I eternally leave the three evil destinies,
May I quickly eradicate greed, hate, and delusion,
May I always abide in Buddha,
Dharma, and Sangha,
May I diligently practice morality,
concentration, and wisdom.

My heart began to fill with yearning. Like waves, like a river, it seeped into my heart, my body, my soul—and spread wider and wider. I gripped the yearning and remembered the faces I knew, one by one. But they each appeared in my mind's eye as lifeless as stuffed animals in a museum.

I shook my head. Through the wide windows of the store, I could see rosaries variously made of cedar, the wood of a bodhi tree, crystal. Some had light-brown beads, some black, all neatly strung.

After looking at the rosaries for some time, I happened to look away and, in that instant, caught a glimpse of a long ash-colored robe hung on a rack in the shop. A shiver ran through my body.

That gray robe... That was Monk Dasol's face, the whisper of the breeze as it touched my heart. That was what I was yearning for.

CHAPTER THREE:

May

After the closing session, I helped the student council decorate the walls of our classroom. With the front wall taken up by a blackboard and large windows for another side of the room, there wasn't a lot of space for the decorations. As limited as it was, it was customary to allocate this space to three subjects: anti-communism, filial piety, and study. But I was a little uncomfortable with the promotion of abstract ideas like anti-communism and filial piety. I didn't believe students could learn anything about these things from looking at faded photographs clipped from old newspapers and magazines. The pictures, once hung up at the beginning of each school year, would stay there through the entire year without being looked at by the students.

I wanted to make better use of the space in my home-room. So, going against school policy and sometimes against the assistant principal himself, I always decorated my classroom how I wanted to, which was to turn the classroom into a small exhibition. I hung works done by my students—paintings, calligraphy, poems—on the walls and changed the display every month. Under each work, I placed a white slip of paper with the title of the work and the name of the artist. Of course, not all of the students participated, but many came to be interested in art. And I didn't expect any artistic masterpieces to be produced, but I valued their efforts in exploring their inner consciousness.

Of the ten paintings that were submitted by the students this month, Hyegang's was best without comparison.

While looking in appreciation at this painting, a harmony of silver gray and dark pink, I felt somebody watching me. Raising my head, I saw Soktae hurry to turn away. His face was grim. I smiled at him in apology because I knew what the expression meant.

"Soktae, is that your work?"

"No." He smiled awkwardly. He was holding a painting behind his back. I could see the tip of a palace.

"It's a landscape. Let me see it."

Soktae reluctantly handed the painting to me. As I looked over it, I could feel the intensity of Soktae's eyes peering at me.

"Did you paint this at Doksu Palace?"

"Yes."

"When?"

"Last Sunday."

"I see. I like how the windows form a pattern here." I smiled at him as I said this, and he relaxed visibly.

The desire for approval is in everybody, but nowhere more strongly than in adolescent students. Girls are incredibly sensitive to who and who is not the teacher's favorite, and from time to time, this causes vicious feuding. Although boys tend to be more generous, there are some boys who are as sensitive as girls.

I was familiar with what happens when a parent or a teacher shows favoritism, so I took care in that respect. But affection is not reasonable; it's determined by emotion, and I have been driven by emotion many times. Today, I was making the mistake of paying more attention to Hyegang, and Soktae's actions put this into sharp relief.

I could feel Soktae's eyes watch me as I helped the students arrange and hang their work on the wall. After finishing, I left the room, pretending that nothing was the matter. But it was a long time before I could stop thinking about the look in Soktae's eyes.

Soktae and Hyegang had been classmates during junior high school and, after graduating from there, happened to be assigned to my homeroom. Soktae was second in the class behind Hyegang, but Hyegang had the better grades by far. There was a ten-point gap between them. As wide as this difference was, Soktae competed fiercely with Hyegang.

All the way home, the thought of Soktae made me uncomfortable. Jaun ran toward me as I got off the bus.

"Hi, Mom."

"Hi, Jaun. Is Doug home?"

"He went out and hasn't come back," Jaun said, holding onto my arm. Then in a sulky voice, she continued, "Mom, I don't like my teacher."

"Why not. You said before you liked him very much."

"My teacher is cheap."

"What? What do you mean by that?"

"He's so cheap, he likes everybody."

I didn't quite know how to respond. "Of course, he does. The teacher should like everybody in the class."

Jaun's small face darkened. "I don't like it. I'm sick and tired of people liking everybody."

"What do you mean?" I asked. "I'm afraid you've lost me."

"My teacher likes Soyoung."

"How's that?"

"Three days in a row, he asked Soyoung to stay after school, and then they went to a doughnut shop to talk."

"Three days in a row? I suspect there's a reason."

"A reason? On Mother's Day, he asked us to write a letter to our moms, and Soyoung began crying because she has no mother. That's it."

"Is that right? That's a big deal, isn't it?"

"When she cried, I felt like crying, too. If the teacher had asked us to write to our dads, I would have cried like Soyoung." Jaun spoke more softly, and her voice was tense.

I tried hard to sound natural. "Then you should be thankful that your teacher is trying to make Soyoung feel better."

"But it makes me mad when he likes somebody more than me." Jaun looked up at me, her eyes brimmed red.

The look stirred me inside. Jaun was looking for a father in her teacher and couldn't stand it that other children could be close to him. Trying to maintain my composure, I hugged Jaun tightly.

"Jaun," I said, changing the subject. "The students in my school are going to East Nine Tomb Park tomorrow for a sketching contest. Would you like to prepare a lunch for Hyegang tonight when we're making mine?"

"Why would we do that?"

"He has no mother to make lunch for him."

"He has no mother?"

"No, and he doesn't have a father either."

"That's so sad. Poor boy." Learning that Hyegang, whom she liked, was worse off than herself, Jaun expressed concern. "Then, where does he live?"

"He's staying with a person who has been raising him."

"That person must be good, too."

I looked at Jaun and smiled. Her cheery look returned. She had forgotten her own misfortune the moment she heard of Hyegang's.

"Which do you like, Jaun, kimchobab or yuchobab?"

"Why?"

"I'll prepare what you like."

"I like kimchobab, but Hyegang might like yuchobab. Why don't we make both?"

After stopping at the market to buy some groceries, we went home. Doug answered the doorbell.

"You've come, Mrs. Kang?" he said in greeting.

"When did you get in? Jaun said you weren't."

"I came in just now."

"I see."

"We should spray the lilacs and the rose bush."

"That's a good idea. There was a problem with insects last year."

"Should I do it now?"

"It's late, isn't it? How about tomorrow?"

"It's not too late. Let me do it now."

I took some money out of my purse and handed it to Doug, who took it and went out whistling happily.

"Damn child. Why is it that he acts like a poisonous serpent only to me?" Dougienei came out, muttering. Probably she had overheard us.

"Aunt Dougienei, it's possible to commit a sin just with what you say. Calling your own son a damn child, what could be a more dreadful sin than that?"

Dougienei's face fell slightly, and taking my lunch box, she went inside.

I went upstairs to change clothes while Jaun chatted with Dougienei in the kitchen, happy to be making lunch for Hyegang. After some time, Doug returned.

"Mrs. Kang," he called.

"Yes? Did you buy the insecticide?"

"Yes, here's the change."

"Are you going to spray it now?"

"Yes. I've heard it's better to do it in the afternoon."

"All right, then go ahead. But take it easy."

"I will." Doug poured the insecticide into the pump and shook it gently before going out into the yard with it.

*   *   *

The sky was clear, and the sunshine was warm. Who was it that compared green leaves in May to the smiles of babies? As it is with all forms of life, the leaves on trees seem most beautiful in their earlier stages, before they mature into a dark green.

The students set up their boards and easels and began drawing diligently. The sketching contest was scheduled for the morning and the composition contest for later in the afternoon.

I sat on a hillside that sloped upwards to one of the tombs. Green shoots of grass grew from beneath the old.

Soon the leaves will disappear and new ones will bud among the tombs. Where did such order begin? It is said that everything goes through four stages: formation, existence, destruction, and annihilation. All things become formed, they abide, they become destroyed, and they become nothing. Nothing, animate or inanimate, is exceptional. I, too, exist and will disappear soon. What meaning can I find while I exist? Am I to be like a leaf, to live only as a small part in nature?

"Mrs. Kang, you look just like a young girl sitting there like that." The fine arts teacher approached, smiling.

"Thanks. Right now, I feel that way."

"What do you think is inside that tomb?"

"Nothing, I imagine."

"Do you believe the soul survives physical death?"

"Yes, I do."

"Then why do you think there's nothing inside?"

"The soul of the person who is buried here must be at least a hundred years old. How could that soul still be in there?"

"That reminds me of Dante's *Divine Comedy*. The most unfortunate souls are those that can go neither to heaven or hell but remain only in empty space."

"I remember that, too. Soul in the vestibule, isn't it?"

"It makes sense to me. If you're not good and you're not evil, that usually means you're completely self-centered, like a seed that can't sprout. You're beyond hope for salvation. So, if you're not going to be good, you might as well be thoroughly evil. Better that than to be lukewarm, don't you think?"

I laughed with him as I stood up. "Will you come with me to see how the students are doing?"

"Sure. Should we go through the woods?"

We walked up the hill.

"I'm feeling pretty cynical about painting these days," the fine arts teacher said.

"Why?"

"There's no real point. It's all pretty meaningless."

"That's not just with painting. Everything in the world is pretty meaningless."

"I agree. There's nothing we can pursue in life. Even Solomon in all his splendor couldn't be like the lilies that grow in the fields."

"Really? Do you think so?" I smiled at him.

"Mrs. Kang, I get the feeling you've achieved some insight into reality that I haven't. Don't you struggle with things in your mind, like I do?

"Do I look enlightened to you?"

"Yes, you do."

"You're kidding. I wish I could have even just a glimpse into what that's like."

"Isn't it being free from passions and delusions?"

"Well, it is said the Chinese poet Tao Yuan-ming once declared, 'Enlightened, I have found nothing in particular; the mountain is still foggy and the ocean is still wavy.'"

"I see. I guess I shouldn't be so discouraged." He laughed.

The budding trees were dazzling to the eye. We had just reached a small stand of trees when the fine arts teacher pointed. "Mrs. Kang, look over there. It looks like Soktae and his friends are picking a fight with Hyegang."

We hurried toward them. When Soktae saw me, he stepped back in embarrassment.

"Is there a problem?" the fine arts teacher asked.

"Nothing," Soktae answered.

"Have you finished your drawing?"

"No, not yet."

"Time's almost up. You'd better hurry." The fine arts teacher looked like he wanted to give Soktae a proper scolding, but I gave him a look that said not to. Instead, we walked away, pretending we hadn't seen anything. Glancing back, I saw Soktae and his friend leave Hyegang alone.

"What was the matter with that fellow?" the fine arts teachers asked.

"He's jealous of Hyegang."

"What a silly kid."

Chapter Three: May

Hyegang came after us down the mountain, his face calm and clear as always. But this time, there was also a trace of suppressed emotion.

"Let me see," the fine arts teacher said to Hyegang, and Hyegang handed him the picture he was holding.

Hyegang turned and looked at me, his eyes full of meaning.

"Hyegang, I brought you a lunch. Jaun worked very hard to make this for you last night. I hope you like it."

Hyegang flushed red, as if all the blood in his body had rushed to his face at that moment. It looked like he wanted to say something, but instead, he accepted the lunch silently with both hands and ran off in the direction of the woods. Watching him, I felt an ache in my heart because I knew, better than anyone else, how sensitive he was to the smallest injury. As I stood there, the fine arts teacher spoke. "Look at this drawing, Mrs. Kang. It's unbelievable!"

I looked at the drawing the fine arts teacher was holding out to me. It was not a picture of trees and tombs, but an expression of colors that suggested them. "It's beautiful," I said.

"This fellow has a gift, an intrinsic sensitivity to beauty," the fine arts teacher gushed.

After lunch, there was the composition contest, which went ahead without incident. Afterwards, I collected the students' manuscripts and arranged them according to class. I was leaving the park with the other teachers when Hyegang ran up to me.

"Mrs. Kang, will you take this for Jaun?" He handed me a drawing, smaller than the one he'd completed earlier but containing the same beauty in color. After giving me the drawing, he ran back to his friends.

The outdoor sketching and composition had gone smoothly as planned, and the day outside in May seemed to have refreshed everyone, students and teachers alike.

I gave Hyegang's drawing to Jaun when I got home.

"This is wonderful, Mom," she exclaimed. "Look at these colors."

"Aren't they nice? All of Hyegang's drawings are like that."

"Mom, would you frame this one for me, too?"

"Of course."

"Mom, do you think Hyegang likes me, too?"

"Of course, he likes you. He would be glad to have a sister like you."

"Do you think so? Then why doesn't he come to visit us more often?"

"He's been very busy. But I'll be sure to invite him when he has some time."

"Please, Mom, invite him soon." Holding the picture with both hands, Jaun went to her room.

Opening session on Monday morning was held in the schoolyard, and during it, there was an awards ceremony for the winners of the sketching and composition contests. Hyegang received first prize for his drawing.

Following the assembly, the phys. ed. teacher led the students through their morning exercises, while the other teachers inspected the students' belongings. During this, the dean of students, who had been looking through my homeroom class, came into the staff room, red-faced. I knew he'd found something but remained silent since nothing had been announced officially.

After the students had returned to their classrooms and taken their places, Hyegang was called in by the dean of students, who kept him well into third period. I could ignore it no longer. I went into the dean's office.

Entering the room, I felt a certain anger surge through me as I saw what reminded me of a cat toying with a mouse.

Hyegang was standing, obviously frightened, while the dean of students held a rod in his hand and sat opposite.

"Excuse me," I said. "May I ask what the matter is?"

Hyegang bit his lip and turned away.

"Good, I was going to discuss this with you," the dean of students said.

"What's the problem?"

"Look at these pictures."

I looked to where he was referring. They were pornographic pictures of naked men and women entangled together. Even though this was not a personal matter, I could feel embarrassment creep over me as I looked at them. But I tried to maintain a calm and business-like approach to the matter, as serious as this was.

"Are these pictures from Hyegang's bag?" I asked.

"Yes, they are. But the fellow denies that they're his."

"That's a little strange, isn't it?"

"What's so strange? If they were in his bag, then they are his."

"As his homeroom teacher, I'd like to look into this a bit further. Would you please keep this incident to yourself for the time being?"

"Well, since it's a request from the homeroom teacher, I'll agree for now. But this kind of thing cannot be allowed to happen with a grade ten student. Once I find out the details, I will impose punishment accordingly."

"I understand. But until we get the full story, let's practice some discretion."

"Fine. I'll keep the pictures, and you can take Hyegang."

"Thank you."

Hyegang followed me wordlessly. I took him to my desk and said, "Hyegang, I know you. And I believe you. Those pictures aren't yours, are they?"

"No, they aren't."

"Do you know how they happened to be found in your bag?"

"I have no idea. I had never seen them before I was called into the dean's office." Hyegang's face paled.

"I understand. I know they're not yours. The rest of the problem is going to take some time to solve."

Hyegang remained silent.

"Attend classes as usual."

"Yes." Hyegang turned and left the staff room.

I was in a dilemma. It was serious enough that a student would be caught having pornographic pictures, but the dean of students, not having forgotten his bad feelings for Hyegang over the incoming assembly, was almost certain to suspend him from school. This could not happen, I decided, not because it would be too much for Hyegang to bear, but because I was aware of the spiritual hurt Hyegang would suffer from the shame.

I examined the matter from different angles, but constantly Soktae's face was in my mind. This had to be his prank. I considered several ways to a solution, but none seemed satisfactory.

An idea didn't come to me until the bell rang for fifth period and my homeroom had gone down to the music room. I would plant the pictures in Soktae's bag and "find" them. I was certain that even though Soktae was able to do something so calculated, he was still a young boy incapable of hiding his feelings.

I went to the dean of students to brief him on my plan and, having got the pictures from him, went back to my classroom. One of the class monitors was absent that day, so only one of the students was there, his head on his desk. I placed the pictures in Soktae's bag and strolled around the room. The student raised his head and saw me only as I was about to leave, probably giving him the impression that I had just walked around to inspect the room.

Discomfort ran through me as I returned to the staff room, as if I had touched filth.

After seventh period, I went to my class for closing session. I led the session as naturally as I could and proceeded to inspect the students' belongings afterwards. I came to Soktae's place after about twenty students. I opened a few books and removed the pictures. Soktae's face went white.

I watched him calmly, as he lowered his gaze, unable to look me in the face. After instructing him to come see me in the staff room after closing session, I continued on to the other students' belongings and finished quickly.

I nervously waited for Soktae in the staff room. Even though he was young, if he was more cunning than I was, he could defeat me. The thought brought some fear with it. I hoped I wouldn't have to resort to extreme measures, in light of the pity and affection I had for Soktae.

Soktae came to me, his frightened eyes searching mine. How those pictures got from Hyegang's bag into his own must have posed a big mystery to him. I pointed to a chair beside me. Soktae sat on it, and after some tense silence, he began to wilt.

"Soktae, as your teacher, I'm here to look out for your best interests. We need to talk honestly now."

Soktae's head hung forward. I could read the shadow of agony cast over his bent shoulders.

"These pictures are yours, aren't they?"

He said nothing.

"Thank you, Soktae. I was worried you might foolishly deny it. Now I can be assured that what you did was a mistake. I'll settle this matter, but when you go home tonight, I would like you to reflect on what you did and know that it was not worthy of a man but cowardly."

"Mrs. Kang, please forgive me." Soktae was completely dejected. He lifted his head and looked at me, his eyes telling me that there was so much more he wanted to say.

"Apologize to Hyegang."

"Mrs. Kang." Soktae began to say something but then let his head drop again.

After Soktae left the room, a feeling of sheer emptiness overwhelmed me. Part of it was because the tension that had been inside of me all day was now released, but mostly, it was because the whole incident had painted a bad picture of human nature for me.

I went to the dean of students' office to return the pictures. The dean was preparing to leave for the day. "Has the problem been resolved?" he asked.

"Yes, as I expected."

"How could that be?" he asked, doubt casting a shadow over his eyes. It was apparent he suspected I would conceal the truth in order to save Hyegang from punishment. "Are you going home now?"

"Yes."

"I'm on my way home, too. Will you join me for a cup of tea?"

"Certainly." I went back to my desk to retrieve my purse and walked out the gate with the dean of students. Uneasiness spread over me. I couldn't be sure how much he was going to believe what I had to say.

We try to communicate through words, but people listening to them seldom accept their meaning as true. They analyze what we say according to their own prescribed definitions and fit them to suit their own interests. Isn't it this miscommunication that is at the heart of our greatest loneliness?

We crossed the street and entered a tearoom called the Lighthouse. The interior was rough, like most tearooms in the area.

"Those pictures were not Hyegang's?" the dean of students began.

"No, they weren't."

"Then who put them in Hyegang's bag?"

"Another student in my class. He was jealous of Hyegang."

"Jealous? Of what?"

"Grades, and things like that."

"That's awful. Who was the awful student?"

Since the waitress came then with our tea, I was able to avoid having to give Soktae's name. "Help yourself to the tea," I said.

"Thank you. Please help yourself, too. It looks like the hollows around your eyes are ten miles deep today." The dean of students laughed pleasantly. Maybe it's human nature to become tender-hearted when there's something to eat and drink in front of us.

"Ten miles? I thought at least twenty miles. I couldn't eat my lunch. It's still in my lunch box."

"You always worry too much about your students. You don't have to be like that. Just do your job, and one year passes. Then you will have nothing more to do with them."

"My character is to blame, I suppose," I said.

"The boy who put those pictures in Hyegang's bag, did he admit to it?"

"Yes. I planted them in his own bag and took them out during inspection. He turned dreadfully white."

"He didn't deny they were his?"

"No, he didn't."

"He has done a bad thing here, but perhaps he is not bad by nature."

"I agree."

"So, what do you think we should do about this matter?" he asked.

"I'm not sure," I replied. "What do you think?"

"So far, nobody knows except you and me, and I'd like to go with what the homeroom teacher decides."

"I appreciate that. If that's how you feel then, let's act as if nothing happened."

"Hyegang has done nothing wrong, so there is nothing to say about him. But do you mean we should let the other one go, too?"

"Yes, please."

"I don't understand."

"If this incident becomes known to others, then he is dead completely."

"That might be true, but…"

"Please, let's forget this. If we say nothing, maybe he will reflect on it on his own and decide never to do such a cowardly thing again. But if we suspend him from school or expel him, and everything comes out into the open, everything will be finished for him."

"You may be right, but it feels somehow incomplete to leave it like this," he said.

"I'm not pleased either. I have to see him every day."

"I understand, though. Punishment is not always the best action."

"Thank you."

The dean of students seemed to have lost his taste for punishment upon finding out that Hyegang was not to be the object of that punishment, and he went along with my suggestion. After paying the bill, I went home. It was fortunate that Hyegang was freed from the trap and that Soktae escaped punishment, but I was not feeling particularly cheerful.

CHAPTER FOUR:
June (I)

The incident with Soktae pushed me into a deep depression. Depression was a chronic condition for me, and I went through bouts cyclically, but if one was triggered by a specific incident, I suffered worse.

I signed the daily report brought to me by a student monitor, and after submitting it to the supervisor, I returned to my desk. The fine arts teacher was watching me. "Mrs. Kang, you're in one of those moods again, aren't you?" he said.

"I beg your pardon?" I asked, surprised.

"I can tell right away when you're depressed."

"How's that?"

"You don't speak at all."

I smiled sheepishly, embarrassed at being unable, even in my thirties, to leave such childishness behind.

"Why are you in charge of weekly duties at a time like this?" the fine arts teacher asked, still looking at me.

"What do you mean?"

"On a day like this, I'd like to take you out for a drink."

"You wouldn't like it. I don't much enjoy drinking."

"What's enjoyable about drinking, except that it gives you a chance to talk?"

"Thank you, but you should probably get home as quickly as you can—before my depression contaminates you."

Sorry that he could not drink with me, the fine arts teacher gave me several quick glances before leaving. The other teachers bustled about, preparing to leave for the day. The staff room gradually emptied, like an ocean bed being swept dry by an ebb tide. The few students in the schoolyard reminded me of small crabs.

Alone in the school building, shrouded in a deep gloomy silence, I leaned back in my chair and closed my eyes. Relaxation is probably in many ways related to loneliness, I thought. I remained there for a long time. My mind released its contents and emptied, and soon became fields, hills, mountains, rivers, and slow-moving clouds against a blue sky. My small body hid in these images, and I sank into a deep, deep rest.

When I opened my eyes, it was half past eight. The teacher on night duty would arrive in thirty minutes. After taking a tour of the hallway to check for open windows, I switched off the overhead lights and went into the extracurriculars room. The whole school was wrapped in darkness, except a sliver of light coming from the fine arts room.

I pushed in through the door and was startled. There was Hyegang, embracing the knees of a statue he had molded. His cheeks were rested against the statue, which was in the image of a woman.

Chapter Four: June (I)

The expression on his face was pure beauty. He looked like a man embracing his love, a baby at its mother's bosom, an animal leaning on the good earth. I held my breath and was quietly making my way out of the room when I heard Hyegang's voice. "Mrs. Kang."

I felt like I'd been caught spying. "I'm sorry. I shouldn't have come in," I said in apology.

"I wanted to see you just now." Hyegang looked at me. His eyes shone with tears.

"You're sculpting someone. Who is it?"

"It's an image of the Bodhisattva the Compassionate."

"The Bodhisattva the Compassionate?"

"Yes."

I remembered our first meeting and the wish he'd expressed then. I looked at the statue. The head was still an oval mass, but the body was beginning to show soft, refined lines. "What will you do with it once you're done?"

"I'll dedicate it to Monk Dasol."

"Monk Dasol?"

"Yes."

"That would be appropriate, since he's the one who led you to the truth of Buddha."

Hyegang said nothing.

"Is Monk Dasol doing well?" I asked.

"Yes, he is. He asked me the same question this morning."

"What question?"

"He asked me if my teacher was well."

I smiled. "Hyegang, it's late. You should go home. Please be sure to turn off the lights and lock the door on your way out."

"I will."

Hyegang scraped chunks of clay off the pedestal and put them into a bucket. Then he wrapped several layers of plastic around the statue, to prevent the air from drying it out. I left the room after Hyegang went to wash his hands.

The teacher on night duty was in the staff room when I returned. "You can go home now, Mrs. Kang. Your duty is over."

I thanked the teacher and left. The mildness of the spring air hung like a soft silk drape in the darkness. Walking across the schoolyard toward the main gate, I could see the school building looming in the black. It looked like a giant sleeping deeply.

Darkness, which gives rest to ten thousand things, is good. The color of death must be like this.

Doug opened the gate when I rang the bell. I got the impression that he'd been pacing in the yard, waiting for me.

"You're still up?"

"Yes."

"You should go to bed."

"It's all right."

Dougienei shuffled out and asked in a sleeping voice, "Where will you take your dinner?"

"I should wash first. Please leave it in the kitchen."

I went upstairs to change and clean up. When I came down, Doug was standing beside the table.

"Why aren't you in bed?"

"He's idling away day and night. How could he possibly fall asleep?" Dougienei remarked. I was so exhausted, I sat down at the table without attempting a response.

"Doug, is there something you want to ask me?"

"No, you look tired."

"I'm not that tired. If you have something to say, take a seat there and talk to me." I pulled out a chair for him.

"Thank you."

"How's it going with the job search?"

"That's what I wanted to discuss with you."

"Go on," I said. "Will you have a cup of tea?"

"Yes, please."

"Auntie, will you make some tea for us?"

Dougienei had been lingering around the table and now went into the kitchen.

"Mrs. Kang, I don't want a job."

"Then?"

"You know, I'm hopeless. What can I aspire to? Money? Power?"

"Well."

"I'm not even interested in those things. What do they mean, money and power?" Doug looked at me cautiously, careful not to make a mistake with his bold statements.

I smiled. "And so?"

"I don't regret that I didn't complete high school or that I didn't attend university."

"I see."

"I believe that it's unfair for me to have been born into this world, but otherwise, I can accept everything and be positive about it."

I remained silent.

"Unfair or not, the fact is I was born, and I should live my life in the right way."

"I see."

"I've been thinking a lot about jobs lately. It seems to me that we have jobs so we can live a good life, but at the same time, the kind of life we have depends a lot on what kind of job we have."

"I agree. The days we spend working make up our lives, too."

"In the past, a man could make his livelihood by becoming a scholar, a farmer, a craftsman, or a merchant. To be a scholar was to be of the highest order, which appeals to me. But also, I know it's unrealistic to think I could be a scholar, so I want to become the next best thing: a farmer. It would be a pure, virtuous life."

I was surprised at his conviction. I knew that Doug was well read in a wide range of subjects, but I hadn't thought that he would have formed such clearly defined views for himself. "I can tell you've thought very deeply about this," I said. "But given the present circumstances, it doesn't sound realistic for you to become a farmer. You have no land or any connection to farming."

"I thought I might study horticulture. I can start at a florist or at a nursery."

"That sounds reasonable. If you're firm in your determination, you should do it."

Doug and I talked some more over tea. He was an adult now, with an adult way of conversation. It was a sharp reminder of how fast time was going by. Time had made this young man out of a little boy. It had also made me into a middle-aged woman.

What power drives all these changes? Nothing in the world—living or non-living—goes unchanged. Does this same power bring harmony to nature?

"Mrs. Kang, you know what life is about, don't you?" Doug asked, looking into my eyes.

"I don't think anybody knows that."

"You seem to know something about life."

"I thought that way when I was young, too—that once a person was grown up, he would know what life meant. But now many years later, I still know nothing about life. Maybe that's what life is."

"Everything seems so vague, and the longer you live, the vaguer they become. Sometimes, you think you can place a finger on what you've been searching for, but then it disappears in the next moment."

I could sense the turmoil going on inside Doug. It made me sad that I couldn't supply him with any answers.

Is this life? Something ugly that can never be found?

"Mrs. Kang, if it's true that we are animals, I think we'd be better off just being animals, thinking of nothing, just eating and reproducing." Doug paused awhile before continuing. "I've been having these cravings these days. Sometimes, it's too strong to control, and I'll abuse myself. But when I look at the semen in my hand, it makes me want to be sick. I want to kill myself. Why is there this contradiction?"

I said nothing. How could I respond? I wish I knew the answer.

"Mrs. Kang, I'm sorry for talking such nonsense."

"Don't be. You can say anything to me if you want to talk. I think talking meets one of our basic needs, too." I smiled at Doug, and he smiled back.

Afterwards, I went upstairs and lay down in my bed.

What is the body? What are its needs? Are they callings from the devil, who is beyond hope for salvation?

The morning air was clear and bright. The fragrance of peony greeted me as I stepped into the yard, and I put my nose to one of the flowers, its yellow stamen peering out from inside dark-pink silk petals. Queen Seondeok of the Shilla Dynasty is said to have thought, after noticing that there were no butterflies near a peony painted on a folding screen, that the flowers had no scent. But this morning, I inhaled, and the scent was as strong as that of any flower.

Doug was already out tending to the garden, and now he approached me. "Mrs. Kang, aren't the wild roses in bloom by this time of year?"

"I think so."

"Of all the flowers, I think wild roses are the most beautiful."

"Maybe because their natural home is in a field."

"Wild roses in bloom have a wonderful scent. Roses are nice, but they're like children from wealthy families and aren't as pretty as wild roses."

"Maybe that's because they grow too close to people. Is there an open field somewhere? A place we could go to where there are no people?"

"A field?"

"Yes, I feel like spending a day in a wide field where there's no one."

"If you go to some place that nobody knows about, I suppose there won't be anybody around."

"Should we go to a place like that on Sunday? It would be a nice change of scene."

Before Doug could answer, Jaun came out into the yard. "Mom, what time did you come home last night?"

"I'm coming home late every day this week because of weekly duties, remember?"

"I tried to wait up, but I must have fallen asleep."

"I'm sorry. But how about a picnic somewhere with Doug on Sunday?"

"That's a great idea, Mom. Can Hyegang come, too?"

"I'll have to ask him."

"Please invite him, Mom."

"I'll ask him at school today. I'll tell him you want him to go with us."

"Good." Jaun pumped my hand up and down a few times and skipped back into the house.

I went in after her and sat down to read the morning paper. My heart began to race when I turned to the culture section. There on the page was Monk Dasol's picture alongside an article titled "The Concept of Emptiness in Buddhism." His eyes in the picture gazed up at me, and emotion filled my heart. I folded the paper carefully and placed it in my bag to read at school.

When I arrived at school, Mrs. Hahn approached me, a severe look on her face.

"What's wrong, Mrs. Hahn," I asked.

"It's so incredible, I can't even say it."

"What?"

"A girl in my neighborhood, a grade ten student at J. Girls' High School, has something to do with your student Soktae."

"Soktae?"

"The girl's mother came to my home last night and informed me her daughter is pregnant."

"What?"

"She demanded that we go to Soktae's house right away. She refused to take no for an answer, and my husband was right there to see it all."

"That must have been hard. Why didn't you contact me?"

"I wanted to, but my husband advised me not to. He thought it would be better to tell you in the morning."

"So, what did the girl's mother say?"

"She said she would like to kill Soktae, and she would like to die with her daughter, too."

Even without having seen her face, I could imagine what kind of state this woman was in. "Mrs. Hahn, why don't you phone the girl's mother now?"

"Fine, but she'll probably call here first."

"If she calls, please let me speak with her. And I'd appreciate it if you wouldn't tell the other teachers about this. I'd like some time to think about how best to handle this."

"There's nothing to think about. Just put the issue on the agenda for the next teachers' meeting and let them expel the boy." Mrs. Hahn's voice was clear and resolute.

"If we do that, the girl's identity may come out and… I think we should give this some serious thought." I could not tell if Mrs. Hahn agreed with this.

The news baffled me. It had been a misery to see Soktae's face ever since that incident with the pornography, and now I had no idea how to deal with this next problem. The telephone rang as I sat restlessly. The vice principal took the call and handed the receiver to me. As Mrs. Hahn expected, the girl's mother had phoned rather than waiting for me to call her.

"Hello," I said.

"Are you Soktae's homeroom teacher?"

"Yes."

"Shame on you. How dare you call yourself a teacher? Do you educate your students, or don't you?"

"Excuse me?"

"You should be thankful I'm not one to curse. What do you teach your students?"

I put my hand on my forehead and bit my lip. The vice principal gave me a look that asked, "What's the matter?"

Before I could say anything else, Mrs. Hahn took the receiver from me and I went back to my desk. I didn't want to think anymore.

After finishing the conversation, Mrs. Hahn came to my desk. "She insisted on coming straight to the school. I had to beg her to meet you at the Lighthouse tearoom."

"Thank you, Mrs. Hahn."

I screwed up the nerve to go to the tearoom and listen to what this woman had to say. I was curious to see what kind of woman she was, and what kind of wisdom lay behind blaming a teacher for her daughter's indiscretion.

I distributed study notes to my class and placed the students under the charge of the class representative before going out to the Lighthouse. Pushing into the teahouse, I saw a woman sitting by the window. She was raising a well-manicured hand.

"I'm Soktae's teacher."

"I knew you were when I first saw you. I'm a master at identifying people."

"Could you give me more details about the problem? I'd like to find a way to solve this." I spoke directly and maintained eye contact. She wilted a little.

"How on earth is this possible?" she said. "These kids, only in tenth grade."

"When did you find out?"

"Yesterday. The damn girl was throwing up, so I took her to the doctor. She's been pregnant for three months, he said."

"Three months? How was it possible for you not to know for three months?"

"I've been busy making a living. I leave her at home, and it was while I was away that she made this horrible mistake."

"On the telephone, you suggested I was to blame. Can you explain?"

"I only said that… well, I was so mad. How is this your fault? These kids—behind our backs—they acted stupidly." She withdrew her previous accusation.

"I'll need to know what school she goes to, what grade she's in, and what class she attends."

"She's in grade ten at J. Girls' High School. I don't know what classroom she's in."

"You don't know the name of her homeroom teacher?"

"I don't know. I'm far too busy to pay attention to that kind of thing."

"What's your daughter's name?"

"Miok, Miok Oh."

"That's everything then. I advise you to deal with this discreetly—the more fuss you make about the problem, the more disadvantage there is to your daughter. If Soktae is expelled from school, your daughter will not be allowed to remain at school either. No school admits pregnant girls." I warned her firmly, and stood up.

Mrs. Hahn came to my desk when I returned to the staff room.

"Do you know her well?" I asked.

"Not very well. She sells black market goods."

"She sells smuggled goods? To you?"

"Yes, she has connections with people in Pusan, and her items are always genuine foreign-made."

"Does she go to Pusan often?"

"More than that. She stays there. It takes a long time to receive the goods from the smugglers, even after the ship has arrived. It's because they need to avoid the customs police."

"Is her daughter's name Miok?"

"Well, she's known as Miok's mom."

"I think I should meet with Miok's teacher, too."

"What are you going to do?"

"Solve the problem. I need to know everything there is to know. It's possible that Soktae is the victim, too."

"That's true. I've heard the girl has a bad reputation."

"How do you mean?"

"Rumor has it that when her mother is out, the girl invites boys to her home and flirts with them."

"I told the girl's mother that I would look into this and get back to her in two or three days. If you see her, would you tell her the same?"

"Certainly."

Mrs. Hahn returned to her seat, but I could tell she was still curious. It nauseated me. The wife of a university professor, she had no qualms about buying smuggled goods. As a teacher, she watched idly by as a student was about to be expelled from school. How did this make sense?

When the bell ending the first period rang, I called Soktae in to see me. He stood in front of me with a deathly pale face. His anguish was clear. I took him to the counseling room on the fourth floor, a green-curtained room that was dark and had an air of stability about it.

"Soktae, this is the last favor I'm doing for you. I'd like for you to accept it."

Visibly frightened, Soktae let his head drop forward.

"How long have you known a girl named Miok?"

He didn't answer.

"Are you rejecting my favor? It's up to you."

"Mrs. Kang, help me, please. These days I can't even walk straight because it feels like this huge mountain is on top of me," Soktae cried.

"I'm trying to help you. That's why we're here. Tell me exactly what happened."

"It was six months ago. I was at home, and a friend of mine from junior high school invited me to get together with some girls he knew."

"So?"

"That was how I met Miok."

"What happened after that?"

"I met her a few times at the doughnut shop, and then she asked me to come to her house. I went there, and nobody was there but us. She acted like a grown-up. She poured whisky into a glass and asked me to drink. I'd never tried whisky before, but I drank it."

"And then?"

"And then Miok took out these pictures and showed them to me. She said they were her mother's. I could feel myself get excited, and my face got all flushed and hot. Then Miok put her arm around my neck, and then I didn't know what I was doing. I..."

"I see. How many times did you see her after that?"

"Three more times. After that, I tried to avoid her."

"When did you see her last?"

"About the end of January."

"You haven't seen her since then?"

"Never."

"How did Miok react?"

"She tried to find me. About two weeks ago, she was waiting for me in front of the school. She told me she was pregnant and said if I didn't meet her, she would tell everything to my parents."

"Two weeks ago?"

"Yes."

"What did you do?"

"I was so scared, I followed her to her house."

"And?"

"I wanted to run away, but I couldn't say no."

"That was when you brought those pictures?"

"Yes."

"Why did you put them in Hyegang's bag?"

"I thought I was ruined. I was jealous that Hyegang was pure."

"Jealous that Hyegang was pure?"

Soktae didn't say anything. After hearing his side of it, I felt pity for him. He'd been deprived of his virginity in such an absurd way. For the first time, I realized that adolescence was difficult for boys as well as for girls.

"I understand, Soktae. I'll meet with Miok. From now on, I hope, you will live up to your place as a student."

"Yes." Soktae checked his crying and left the counseling room. I lingered for a while afterwards, leaned back in the sofa. The school bell signaled the start and end of classes, but I lacked the energy to get up. Once again,

I knew that life was a maze. I left the counseling room at lunchtime.

In the staff room, I went to the fine arts teacher. "Could I ask a favor?"

"Name it."

"I have to do something for one of my students, so I have to leave early. Could you cover for me on weekly duties?"

"No problem. I only have to stay until five because it's Saturday, right?"

"Yes."

"That's fine. I have nowhere to go anyway. And it's a good chance to daydream as much as I want."

"Dream that you're a world-famous master painter."

"I will. Nobody will tangle with me in that dream." He laughed cheerfully.

I approached Mrs. Hahn to ask if she would accompany me to Miok's house. With the principal being away, there was no closing meeting, so after compiling the weekly attendance for my class and submitting it, I left with Mrs. Hahn.

"Miok's house is close to yours?"

"Only a few houses down."

"How long does it take to get there by bus?"

"About thirty minutes."

"Let's take a taxi."

"All right. You look so tired today."

"Do you think Miok will be at home?"

"Probably she is. After yesterday's bout, she should be, anyway. Why don't you phone first?"

"I was worried that Miok would leave the house if she knew I was coming, and I don't trust her mother very much either."

"You may be right."

The taxi dropped us off in front of Mrs. Hahn's house, beside Sajik Park.

"Would you like to come in for a cup of coffee before we go on?"

"No thanks. I'm not much in the mood for that."

Mrs. Hahn laughed. "You look just like a soldier on his way to the battlefield."

"Do I really?"

"Yes, you do. As tense as you are, you could be a boy hero going to conquer the castle of the horned devil."

"You just said I looked like a soldier."

She laughed. "Same thing."

I laughed with Mrs. Hahn. It did feel like I was going on an adventure, to challenge people whom I didn't understand.

When Mrs. Hahn rang the bell at Miok's house, a girl answered the door.

"Mrs. Kang, you're in luck. This is Miok."

"Thank you," I said.

"I'll go then," said Mrs. Hahn. "After you're finished, why don't you drop in at our house. I'll brew up some coffee."

After Mrs. Hahn left, I turned my attention to Miok. I studied her face carefully. It looked too jaded for her to be just a teenager. There were dark shadows around her eyes, and her lips were thick and bluish.

"I'm Soktae's teacher. Is your mother in?"

"Yes, she is." Miok hesitated a moment before going into the house. I could hear the bustle of visiting women inside.

"Who was that?"

"Soktae's teacher."

"What? She said she wouldn't be here for a couple of days. Why is she here now?"

"Who's Soktae's teacher?" another voice broke in.

"You don't have to know."

"Damn it, right at the climax—all steamed out!"

"I'll give you a better massage later."

I stood there feeling a little dizzy. The door opened, and Miok's mother poked her head out. "What are you here for?"

"I have some things to discuss with you."

"Come in."

As I stepped onto the porch, the women inside the house one by one poked their heads out the door to take a look at me. The door was slightly ajar, and through the narrow opening, I could see pornography spread out on the floor and a small movie projector on a table.

"I have friends over. We'd better talk out here." Miok's mother pointed to the chairs on the porch.

"That's fine."

"Will you have a drink?"

"No, I'd like to finish with this business."

"Business? So, you've decided how to deal with that damn kid?"

"We've decided to expel him."

"Is that all?"

"I'm only his school teacher. What else can I do?"

"Then what brought you here?"

"I need a signature from you confirming Miok's pregnancy."

"What do you need that for?"

"For the student's expulsion, your daughter's identity must be known."

"To whom?"

"To the board of teachers at our school and at your daughter's."

"Miok's school, too?"

"Yes." This was an empty threat, of course. There was no requirement to inform Miok's school of the incident, but the tactic was possible because Miok's mother was uninformed.

"Mom, this can't get out at my school."

"Girl! You be quiet." Miok's mother snapped at her daughter, then turned in the direction of her friends in the house, as if to solicit their help.

"What's the problem out there?" one of the women called, peering out the door.

"This stupid girl got herself pregnant."

"Splendid!" The women inside burst into laughter.

"You have company. I should go," I prompted. "Please sign here."

"What's she saying now?"

"She says that they have to know Miok is pregnant if they want to kick the guy out of school."

"Who're they?"

"The teachers at the boy's school and at Miok's."

"If the teachers at Miok's school find out about this, do you know what would happen? They'd kick her out."

"That's what I'm thinking, too."

"Forget it. Forget it. Let her have the chance to at least get her high school diploma."

"That's right. If she gets kicked out now, there's only one place for her to go."

Each woman in the room had something to say about the situation.

"Does this mean we can't get anything from the boy's parents?" This is what seemed to have been the intention all along. It was intolerably disgusting.

I turned directly to Miok. "You saw Soktae in January didn't you?"

"Yes."

"And you've been pregnant three months now."

She didn't answer.

"There's something wrong about this, isn't there?" I continued.

The women in the room burst into another round of laughter. "Girl, you're so young. How can you not know who the father of your baby is?" Another voice chimed in, "This is too much. Absolutely!"

While the comments came streaming out of the room, Miok broke. "Because Soktae was avoiding me."

The issue was settled. "I think I'd better go," I said. I left the noisy women and came out into the street. It was nauseating to think that those women and I were of the same species, with a body and standing on two feet on the same earth.

After walking awhile, I came to the long clay wall that bordered Sajik Park. I leaned against it, looking up at the sky. It was colored with purple clouds, lit by the setting sun. I watched for a long time as the pollution shed from my body.

Nature is beautiful.

I walked further, and as I arrived at Anguk district's main intersection, the stores in front of Chogye-sa Temple came to mind.

Browsing at one of the stores, I could hear the recitation of the *Thousand Hands Sutra*.

> When I go to the boiling hell,
> May I help to destroy it.
> When I go to the dungeons of hell,
> May I help to empty them.
> When I go to the hungry ghosts,
> May I lead them to satiation.
> When I go to the beasts,
> May I have the wisdom to help them.

As the sonorous sounds mingled with the steady beat of a wooden bell, I stood there, listening. It felt as if I were at a temple deep in the heart of the mountains. My heart stilled to embrace the sounds, and loneliness swept through my body. A vague yearning. Then I heard a soft voice: "Why are you here, Mrs. Kang?"

It was Monk Dasol.

"What has brought you here, Monk Dasol?" I asked, trying to regain my composure. The unexpected encounter had flustered me.

"I'm here to deliver a lecture at Chogye-sa Temple."

"A lecture? May I sit in?"

"Of course." He smiled. Looking into his gentle eyes, I knew I'd been waiting for him.

"I've never been to the temple. Do we go through this alley?"

"Yes, it's almost time. Shall we go?"

Monk Dasol led me to the temple. In the courtyard grew a big zelkova tree, and under this tree, doves pecked at their food. The place was so peaceful and still, it was hard to believe we were in the middle of a city.

Several students were standing at the entrance of the hall, waiting to usher Monk Dasol in. I followed and took a seat at the rear of the hall.

After performing a few rites, Monk Dasol began the lecture. "… In the Buddhist scripture, there is a saying: 'Proceed beyond the stage of the common people to achieve the stage of no-return and be born in the house of the Buddha.' The stage of the common people, as you may know, refers to the realm of consciousness through which we view everyday existence. And to transcend this realm means to extinguish it.

"To extinguish our realm of consciousness is not to suggest that there is to be absolute nothingness, however. For beyond our everyday existence, there emerges a completely new dimension of the world. So, in one way, extinguishing ordinary consciousness might be referred to as absolute nothingness. But seeing it in another way, we might call this dimension truth itself, the house of the Buddha—the state of the bodhisattvas destined to attain the Buddhahood....

"The ten stages of the bodhisattvas refer to the ten steps of spiritual development. The first step is to achieve joy, which comes with realizing truth. The second..."

Listening to Monk Dasol define the ten stages of the Buddhahood, I arrived at the understanding that true knowledge of the universe could come only from proceeding through these stages. It was only natural that I would have the questions I did.

The chairman struck a bamboo rod against the floor three times when Monk Dasol had finished speaking, and the students fell into meditation. I closed my eyes. In my mind's eye, I saw the figure of Buddha, and before it, there was I, kneeling.

I waited for Monk Dasol in front of the temple after the session ended. "Monk Dasol, I'd like to buy you a cup of tea," I said when he came out.

"That would be nice."

We went into the Bodhi Tree teahouse nearby.

"I was listening to your lecture this evening, and for the first time in my life, Buddhism touched my heart," I told him.

"That's very fortunate. Perhaps you had a special relationship with Buddha's truth in your previous lives."

"Previous lives?"

"All sentient beings transmigrate through six realms of existence: heavenly being, human being, fighting spirit, hungry ghost, animal, and hellish being. The progress of this transmigration is determined by the karma one has accumulated up to that point. If you've had a special relationship with Buddha's truth, and studied it diligently, you would start now from that."

"Where are these six realms?"

"In our minds maybe."

"In our minds?"

"Yes, but in my mind, these realms seem to be hidden. How about in your mind, Mrs. Kang?" Monk Dasol's eyes danced.

"In my mind, too, mostly," I said. "But it's agonizing to find that there is more hell for me than there is heaven."

"I'm sorry to hear that. You'd better enter the ten stages of the bodhisattva as soon as you can," he joked mildly.

"What is the bodhisattva state?"

"It's the state in which you seek to worship Buddhas above you while leading those below you toward salvation. It's through this you attain the state of Buddha."

"Isn't it possible to save beings only after you've gone through the stages of the bodhisattva yourself?"

"That's true, but even as we pass through these stages—and in spite of our shortcomings—we should try to help our fellow peers." Monk Dasol paused for a moment before continuing, "The most important thing is to practice. You can know things theoretically, but until you put them into practice, what good are they?"

"I know what you mean. Many times, I've failed to act as I teach to my students."

"That's not specific just to you. That's the case with me, too." Monk Dasol was as frank about his human side as he was at our last meeting.

I looked at him, thinking, "This man is honest." The thought made me trust him more. As Monk Dasol sat quietly, his hands folded on his knees, I sensed the flow of energy, clearly as a perfect halo, that moved over him.

Monk Dasol is like a pine tree standing by itself deep in the mountains. I didn't know why I felt this the moment I first saw him.

CHAPTER FIVE:
June (II)

"Summer has really arrived, hasn't it?" the geography teacher said, yawning deeply. "I'm terribly drowsy every afternoon these days."

"Yes, it sure is summer. We're in the middle of June already."

"We're going to have a hard time from now on. Drowsiness will make these students duller than they already are."

"That must be especially true in your class."

"Why do you think so?"

"You don't teach something interesting like geography, but that terrible math."

"You think geography is interesting? Ha. It seems to me geography is the true symbol of world-weariness. Just the mention of it is enough to put me to sleep."

"Why do you hate geography so much?"

"My geography teacher had a nose like a Jew. I don't know if he really worked for the GIs, but all he talked about was butter and cheese."

"What do butter and cheese have to do with geography?"

"He didn't talk about ordinary butter and cheese. He would say, 'You can't eat butter if it's rotten, but that's not true for cheese. All you have to do is rub it against your pants.'"

"What does rubbing it against your pants do?"

"I don't know. While he was explaining, I fell asleep."

The teachers in the staff room had a laugh over this.

"You don't need to bother these sleepyheads with logarithms, factors, and all that stuff."

"Why not?"

"It's useless, obviously. I've lived this long, and I've never applied what I learned in math class except addition, subtraction, multiplication, and division."

"Ha. Then I suppose I should pull my son out of school once he's done grade three."

"Sure. He can write love letters. He'd miss nothing."

"I'd hoped for my son to get a doctorate degree. I guess I should reconsider."

"What are you people over there being so noisy for? This is a good example of why teachers should never be idle," the chemistry teacher chided.

"Idle? We would prefer to be teaching. I was just in charge of weighing the boys, and now I have a headache from the stink of their feet."

This delivered another round of laughter. The teachers were enjoying the off-time together. The morning had been busy with the boys' physicals. In the afternoon, doctors had come in to complete the check-ups, so there were no classes.

While the teachers chattered on, the thought going through my mind was this question of whether life had dignity in its nature. If it did, then its conception must also have its dignity. Yet I could not conclude that the act of conceiving life was a dignified one. The Soktae incident had added to my skepticism. A life in Miok's belly, the faces of those women—can we really confer dignity on these?

"What's on your mind, Mrs. Kang?" The school nurse came to where I was.

"I'm just sitting."

"Could you come with me, please? The doctors would like to speak with you about one of your students, Myongkyu."

"The doctors?"

"Yes."

I went with the nurse to the infirmary. There, a ruddy-faced doctor asked if I was Myongkyu's teacher.

"I'm his homeroom teacher. Is there something wrong with him?"

"His homeroom teacher should know, shouldn't she?" the doctor asked his colleague, who was standing beside him.

The colleague agreed.

"What's the matter?" I asked impatiently. The doctor began to say something, then happened to look at the nurse.

"Is my being here a problem?" she asked.

"I'm sorry, but this is a matter that needs to be handled with some discretion."

"I understand. I'll leave."

"I'm sorry."

"Not at all." The nurse left the room.

"What's the matter?" I repeated.

"What does Myongkyu's father do for a living?"

"I believe he's a doctor."

"What does he specialize in?"

"Well, I've never met him, so I'm not sure. I just remember reading in his student profile that his father was a doctor."

"I presume we can find his home phone number on his student profile?"

"Yes, but what is the matter?"

"This is serious. Have you noticed anything peculiar about Myongkyu lately?"

"Peculiar?" I had no clue what he was talking about.

"Myongkyu has no sensation around his spinal column."

"What does that mean?"

"We'll have to conduct some more tests, but at this point, it looks to us like the beginning stages of leprosy."

"What?" My hands went to grasp the back of the chair.

"Don't be overly concerned. We'll need to conduct some more tests to be sure."

"Leprosy is incurable, isn't it?"

"That's not true. If found early enough, it's easily curable. Even severe cases are treated with successful results these days."

I returned to the staff room and wrote down the name and phone number of Myongkyu's father on a slip of paper. Back in the nurse's room, I handed the slip to the doctor, who left saying that he would inform the school as soon as they knew anything. After they left, I went back to my desk and sat in my chair. I stayed there for a long time.

Life was a series of conflicts. A virus that eats away at the human body—was this the breath of the devil? Can we escape the devil even as we keep our physical body?

"Mrs. Kang, is there anything to tell the students before they go home?" the fine arts teacher asked.

"I don't think so."

"I should remind them to pay their tuition. That's something we should do every day." The fine arts teacher picked up his notebook and left his seat. I felt I should follow suit but couldn't manage it. It felt like a wind was blowing against my weak body. How could I fight it?

Finally, and after much effort, I stood up and walked out of the staff room. The staircase up to the third floor where my classroom was looked like a long way up.

Myongkyu's face caught my eye as I pushed into the classroom. His features were well-defined and fairly complexioned.

Looking at his handsome face, I prayed inside that the doctors were wrong in their suspicions. Even famous doctors misdiagnosed. Certainly, this doctor could have been wrong. The cruelest fate would not let an innocent body decompose alive, would it?

I asked the students to sing "Thinking of a Friend" and looked over the classroom while they sang. Hyegang's seat was empty. When the students finished the song, I asked why Hyegang was absent.

"Hyegang has become a living Rodin," Changho volunteered.

"What do you mean?"

"I mean this." Changho put his fist under his chin and posed like Auguste Rodin's *The Thinker*.

I smiled at the reference and asked, "Where is he?"

"He's under the maidenhair tree over by the night-duty room."

"Since when?"

Myongkyu spoke up carefully. "During the physical, I asked him something, and he made a strange face and went to the maidenhair tree."

After class, I asked Myongkyu to come see me. "What did you ask Hyegang?" I asked.

"During the physical this afternoon, the doctor tapped me on the back with a rubber hammer and asked if I felt anything. When I said no, the doctor shook his head."

"So?"

"Afterwards, I asked Hyegang if he'd felt anything when the doctor was hitting him with the rubber hammer."

"What did he say?"

"He said it hurt. So I said, 'That's strange. I felt nothing.' Then he went to the maidenhair tree, and he's been there ever since."

"I see. Thank you. You can go home now. Your father will be waiting for you."

"Goodbye." Myongkyu left the room, not suspecting anything.

I wanted to go to Hyegang but went back to the staff room instead. What could I say to him? Could I say that everything is determined by fate, that his father's situation was determined by fate? Could this be any consolation to Hyegang now?

I felt helpless, like a defeated soldier returning from the battlefield. There was nothing I could offer Hyegang, except to tell him that my heart ached for him. But even this was nothing in the face of his suffering. How sharp the nature of human finitude.

How great are those who can transcend this finitude. They are the stars that twinkle in the night sky and the flowers that scent the mountain meadows. And to think, of these great souls who successfully achieve transcendence, only the greatest achieve sainthood. These are the people, who, like the sun and the moon, can share their light purely.

One who can encourage and console the suffering, the lonely, and the desperate; one who can transcend space and time to save all souls—this person deserves our eternal admiration and adoration.

There was a note from Myongkyu saying he would be absent from school for some time. I was confident that his father, a doctor, would ensure that he received the best possible treatment. But each time I entered the classroom to find his seat empty, I prayed for his quick recovery. For several days, this was my all-consuming hope.

During this time, Hyegang went about his work with a dim expression on his face, like that of a sleepwalker. It was painful to watch him in this state, especially because there was nothing I could do for him.

Summer came like a fresh breeze. The trees in the schoolyard shone green. The sight of them reminded me of the promise I'd made to Jaun. I longed to see open fields and surround myself in nature, to be like a tree and breathe it all in.

During lunch hour one day, the fine arts teacher called Hyegang to the staff room to go through the procedures involved in the after-hours management of the fine arts room. Hyegang stood, not an expression on his face and obviously not hearing a word of what the fine arts teacher was saying.

"Hyegang, listen!" the fine arts teacher erupted finally. "What's the matter with you? I'm finished. You can go."

Hyegang bowed to the teacher and turned to leave. After a few steps, he paused and directed his gaze at me, his eyes brimming with questions. I knew what he was asking. Without a doubt, he wanted to know about his parents. But I couldn't meet his gaze. I could never assume the responsibility of telling him the truth.

Hyegang's face twitched slightly.

"Hyegang," I said, my voice quivering. "Would you like to visit the countryside with us this Sunday?"

"The countryside?"

"Yes, Jaun wanted me to invite you."

"I'll ask Monk Dasol." He went out of the staff room quietly.

On Saturday afternoon, I went grocery shopping with Jaun in preparation for the picnic.

"Mom, do you think Hyegang will bring his drawing supplies?" Jaun asked as we unpacked the groceries. She had been excited ever since hearing that Hyegang was going to join us for the outing.

"I didn't mention it."

"Oh, you should have! I'd like to see him draw."

"Well, maybe he will, if he feels like drawing."

"Where will we go, Mom?"

"Well, the better-known places will be crowded. How about going to the train station and picking the destination that sounds best to us?"

"Do they have the names of the places at the station?"

"Of course."

"That sounds like fun."

"Mrs. Kang, who is Hyegang?" Doug asked, having overheard us.

"He's one of my students. Jaun likes him very much."

"Oh, now I see why Jaun is always talking about him," Doug teased.

"Doug, you're telling lies about me." Jaun glared at Doug.

"Lies?" I joined in. "No, even with me, you always seem to want to talk about Hyegang."

"Mom, you, too?" Jaun stomped into her room.

"Mrs. Kang," Doug said after Jaun had left. "I've applied with the experimental farm at K. University. I start next month."

"K. University?"

"Yes."

"I hear they have an excellent agricultural sciences program. What will you study?"

"I'd like to learn about horticulture, floriculture especially."

"Growing flowers?"

"Yes."

"To spend life growing flowers, that sounds like the life of angels."

Doug remained silent, but his face was set with determination.

"I used to think this way," I continued. "If there is a hierarchy to plants, flowers must be of the highest order. Their beautiful colors, shapes, and fragrances—how could they not be?"

Doug listened attentively.

"In Buddhism, there is something called the flower offering," I said.

"They offer flowers to the Buddha, don't they?"

"Right. In this book I read, it says that when Buddha attained enlightenment, flowers rained down on him from the cloudless heavens in celebration."

"That sounds fantastic."

"Doesn't it?" I agreed. "I don't know if this is why it originated, but now there is a Buddhist ritual called the scattering of the flowers. You scatter flowers in front of the Buddha as you pass by."

"They have such highly elaborate rituals in Buddhism, don't they?"

"Flowers, I believe, are a highly evolved form of life. Living among them, what more could you expect?"

"Listening to this, I'm more confident in my decision." Doug smiled. How could his wandering soul have found a home in flowers?

"Will you be staying at the farm then?"

"Yes, I have a place at the greenhouse. When I think about it, my heart races. Flowers give us beauty, but they require our love. I'll love them dearly."

"How are you going to live in a greenhouse?"

"There's a small room attached to it. I'll use it as a kitchen and bedroom."

"Do your best. You have good intentions, and I'm sure you'll be successful."

"Thank you, Mrs. Kang."

I advised Doug not to stay up too late and went to my room. I was grateful to see that he was trying to lead a right and meaningful life.

The sky in the morning was clear. I prepared lunch with Dougienei, wrapping the rice into little rolls. I was in a happy mood and, like a restless child, looked forward to seeing open fields. It had been a long time.

We had finished making the rolls and were preparing drinks when Hyegang came in. He was wearing pants and a blue T-shirt. Slung over one of his shoulders was his easel.

"Mom, Hyegang brought his drawing supplies!"

"You were wishing for that last night. Maybe Hyegang heard."

"How could Hyegang have heard my thoughts?"

"They say that between people who are very close to each other, thoughts can be spoken without words."

Hyegang smiled.

The drinks prepared, we left Dougienei to go about her household chores and left the house with our packed lunch.

"Mom, look how clear the sky is!"

"Yes, it's very refreshing."

"It feels like when we would go picnicking during grade school," Doug said.

"That was a good time?" Jaun asked.

"Yes, happy."

"Why?"

"Maybe because I liked the lunches."

"It was good because of the food?"

"Well, what do you like about picnics, Jaun?"

"I guess you're right. That's the only thing I like about them, too. Every year, we go to the same place and it's always so crowded, there's hardly anywhere to sit."

Children in Seoul, how poor they are. To those of us who were raised in the countryside, it's as if they are in prison.

After a short ride in a taxi, we arrived at Seoul Station. It was already filled with people. Where were all these people coming from and where were they going?

"Here we are," I said. "Look up there at the names of the train stations and pick one that sounds most interesting."

The three faces peered up at the board.

"Cheongsol sounds good to me." Hyegang spoke first.

"Cheongsol?" I said. "I guess it means 'green pine,' except *cheong* is a Chinese word and *sol* is a Korean word. That's an interesting compound."

"Cheongsol sounds much better than Cheongsong. Maybe that's why they made it like that."

"Mom, that sounds like a nice place." Jaun shook my arm. "Let's go there."

"How's it sound to you?" I looked at Doug.

"That's fine with me," Doug agreed.

We bought four tickets for Cheongsol, an hour and twenty minutes from Seoul Station. We waited until the gates opened, then hurried down the steps and boarded. It had been a long time since I'd been on a train.

There is something romantic about traveling by train. It breaks the bonds that come with day-to-day living. And isn't that freedom in its truest form? True freedom, I think, can be gained only by giving up everything. That means giving up not just what we have, but also our desires for what we want. What could be a greater freedom than this? Indeed, as Meister Eckhart, a German mystic, once said to the effect that the aim of life is to gain freedom which can be gained only by giving up our selfish desires.

Caught in the web of hopes and desires, however, the human soul is fated not to enjoy such freedom. As it is, we live without knowing there is a blue sky above our heads. And to think how trivial and petty are these desires that bind us. It's true, we are dumb animals that struggle and die in self-laid traps.

"Mrs. Kang, what are you thinking?" Doug asked.

"I was wondering why I lived so long without taking this trip."

"You're busy making a living, just like everybody else."

"Yes, we're all busy making a living. But the point is, nobody is forced to live like that."

Doug agreed with me, but as young as he is, he probably didn't fully understand. To change the subject, I said, "We should be seeing the countryside once we get past Suwon, shouldn't we?"

"I'm not sure. I've never been this way."

"Mom, the car is rocking so much. We're sure going fast, aren't we?"

"We really are."

"How can such a big train run on such slim rails?"

"I'm wondering that, too."

"Hyegang, do you ride the train a lot?"

"No, this is my first time."

"You've never been on a train before?"

"No." A shadow of loneliness crossed Hyegang's face. He must have been thinking about how he had never had anyone to take him on a trip or anyone for him to visit.

"We're already far from the city. I feel better," Doug said, looking out the window. "Look at that barley field. So that's why they call them golden waves."

"Where? Where's the barley field?" Jaun asked, craning her neck.

"Over there, can you see the yellow field by that hill over there? That's barley."

"It's yellow because it's ripe, right?"

"What beautiful colors," I said, looking at Hyegang.

"Yes, very. Most of nature is green, and I think that color gives us a glimpse into perfect beauty."

"If green were created by a person, it wouldn't be nearly as beautiful."

"I think so, too. When I paint, it always feels like there's something missing in the colors. I don't think there's life in them."

"It's true. Even the greatest artist can't express life in its purest form."

"I think it's probably impossible. Life is only in nature, in the universe, and in truth."

I said nothing further and looked at Hyegang. For a student in tenth grade, he had surprisingly deep insights.

"Mom, look, they're transplanting the rice, aren't they?" Jaun asked, pointing to some farmers in a paddy.

"You're right, but you didn't even know what a barley field was. How do you know about rice planting?"

"I saw a picture like that in my social studies book."

We laughed. But also I was taken aback by the thought that Jaun was like a plant, growing up through a crack in the pavement. The source of all life is nature. These children are growing up so far away from it!

"Mrs. Kang, three more stations, and then we'll be there," said Doug, looking at the map on his knees.

"That close already?"

"Yes, we passed Suwon quite some time ago."

"The train is going too fast. I wish it would slow down a bit."

The children laughed at what I said, but I think they felt the same way.

We passed through a field of green, and here and there in it were brick houses, eyesores, as far as I was concerned, but I had no intention of dwelling on it. That we had escaped Seoul made me happy.

The Cheongsol station was not very tall, as was the case with most rural train stations. Close to the building grew a dense thicket of juniper trees. In front of the building, there was a small cluster of two- and three-story buildings and a row of shops.

We did not go into the town but instead took a road that led us to a creek. From both sides of the creek, vast fields spread out, and in the distance, at the foot of some hills, there was a small hamlet.

"Mom, the water is really clear, isn't it?"

"Yes, it is. Probably the people in that village can wash their vegetables in here."

"And not have to wash them again when they get home?"

"Of course."

"It must be wonderful to live here." Jaun looked around.

"Hyegang, where should we go? You're the artist, so you're probably best qualified to choose," I said.

"How about those hills over there? We can probably get there by following this stream," Hyegang said, pointing to the mountain at the opposite end of town. There was a thick forest growing up the side, probably giving the town its name.

"What do you think, Doug? Should we go this way?"

"The pine trees look nice."

We walked along the stream. White storks glided overhead, their wings outstretched, as they looked for frogs. It was ironic to think that their beautiful movements were being made in preparation for killing.

After a distance, we came to an old-fashioned bridge made of narrow logs and boards.

"What's that, Mom?" Jaun pointed to the logs.

"That's a bridge."

"How can a bridge be so narrow?"

"In the olden days, people used that kind of bridge."

"How about cars?"

"In those days, cars were rare. Everybody used A-frames."

"But how could they carry all their things over this bridge without falling?" Jaun looked at the bridge, wide-eyed.

"It's been a long time since I've seen a bridge like this," Doug said. "When I was little, there was one near my grandparents' house. I'd always get dizzy crossing it and would have to crouch down and hold on."

"It was like that for me, too," I said. "When the wind made a ripple in the water, it was like the whole bridge was floating away." Doug and I laughed over our memories.

This bridge was in such bad shape, it was doubtful whether we could cross it. Years of rain and wind had worn away at it so that now the logs were rotted and dark. Some of the boards were missing, and there were gaps here and there.

"It doesn't look like people go this way anymore," Doug said half to himself as he looked around. "But there isn't any other way to get across."

"Mom, why don't you ask that man over there?" Jaun said. She was pointing to a man down the creek, digging a ditch at the bank.

I started to go when Doug volunteered and trotted over to the man. After exchanging a few words, he came back, disappointment on his face.

"Mrs. Kang, the man said we shouldn't cross that bridge."

"Why not? The bridge is too weak?"

"No, that's not the reason. He said that hamlet is for lepers in remission."

"Lepers?"

"Yes, he said there are about fifteen houses. They're at the hog pen working right now, so there'll be no one there."

"I don't see any houses."

"Probably they're just huts, too small to see from here."

"Mrs. Kang, lepers don't have eyebrows, do they?" Hyegang asked suddenly. His face was tense.

"No, they don't," I answered cautiously.

"And they have no feeling in their body?"

"When the leprosy spreads to their bodies, that's true."

Hyegang's face showed his agony. Thoughts whirled in my head. How was I going to bear this? "Doug will you take Jaun over that way? It looks like there's a pond over there."

"What about Hyegang?" Jaun asked, but then seeing Hyegang's face, she followed Doug without saying anything further.

"Mrs. Kang, you know about my parents, don't you?"

"Your parents?"

"You've heard about my parents from Monk Dasol."

"From Monk Dasol?"

"I've been attending school for ten years now. You're the first teacher he has ever met."

I said nothing.

"Mrs. Kang, my parents were lepers. I can remember."

I didn't have the heart to look into his face. Helplessness overwhelmed me.

"Mrs. Kang, I've been trying to remember my parents—like an animal left alone in the wild, sometimes looking around, sometimes smelling around. I wanted to know that I was a son and that I was given birth to by parents."

I looked at Hyegang and at the loneliness that stood over him. An animal left alone in the wild.

"Hyegang, come here. Come and hold my hand."

Hyegang collapsed into my arms and cried into my chest. "Mrs. Kang, you are the good earth for me, the good earth which embraces everything," he sobbed.

Yes, I want to be the good earth for you, the good earth where you can strike your roots and grow tall.

Hot tears flowed in my heart.

CHAPTER SIX:

July (I)

Hyegang sank into a deep depression after our trip to Cheongsol. His face remained serene as always, but underneath it all, he must have been struggling terribly, conflict whirling in his heart like dregs in water.

Seeing Hyegang like this prompted me to call on Monk Dasol. I thought he should know that Hyegang remembered his parents and knew what happened to them. Also, I needed someone to share this burden.

I telephoned Monk Dasol late in the afternoon. He answered in a quiet voice. "Hello?" My heart beat faster.

"How are you, Monk Dasol? This is Hyegang's teacher."

"Oh yes. How are you, Mrs. Kang? Is there something I can help you with?"

"I'm wondering if we could meet to discuss Hyegang."

"Certainly. What time would be convenient for you?"

"If possible, I'd like to see you today."

"That would be fine. Shall we meet at the Bodhi Tree?"

I returned to my desk after hanging up, feeling anticipation in my chest. I arranged my desk quickly and left the staff room.

The July sun was unbearably hot. "I wish we could cut half of that sun and shine it in winter," I thought childishly as I walked toward the bus stop. At the stop, there were five or six boys from my class.

"Why are you still here?" I asked.

"It's too hot to ride in the bus," one boy answered.

"Mrs. Kang, it sure is a hot and thirsty day, isn't it? If only I could get rid of this thirst," another offered.

I laughed because I knew what they were getting at. "Where do you want to go?"

"Over there. There's an excellent place over there."

I followed the boys to this excellent place. It was a small shop, a bamboo shade hanging in the window. The boys moved around the place with a familiar air. They greeted the owner with winks as they seated themselves around a table.

"What will you have?" I asked.

"A snow bowl, please."

"Mister, could you give these boys a snow bowl?"

"Yes, ma'am."

The man placed a lump of ice on a small machine painted in blue. The machine began spinning the lump, and underneath, powdered ice gathered in a bowl like soft snow. He let the machine run until the bowl was heaping full of ice. On top of this mound, he spooned a generous portion of sugared red-bean mash and topped this with syrup. It was apparent the boys thought this place was excellent for its generous portions.

"Dig in, then go home once you're finished."

"How about you, Mrs. Kang?"

"I have to go."

I left after paying the bill, the boys saying "thank you" with ice-filled mouths.

Inside the bus, it was hot and sticky and very uncomfortable. I got off at Jongno, the street flooded with people. Thrust into this mass of humanity, I thought of what the Buddhists call "scorching hell." I wondered if there were this many people in scorching hell.

I wiped sweat off my face with a handkerchief as I opened the door into the Bodhi Tree. It was air-conditioned inside, and the cool air felt like paradise. Monk Dasol was waiting for me at a table by the window. I walked toward him, apologizing for being late.

"I've only been here a few minutes."

"I'm sorry you had to come downtown on such a hot day."

"You had to come, too, didn't you?"

We laughed about this and eased over some pleasantries before I brought up the reason why I had called.

"Have you noticed any change in Hyegang lately?" I began.

"Has he learned about his parents?"

"You knew about it?"

"It was just a guess."

I related the details of what had happened in Cheongsol.

After waiting for me to finish, he said, "It must have come as a shock to the boy. But if the law of causation was at work, it is natural that he should know." I reflected on this while he continued, "I have been raising Hyegang under the belief that I was fated to have a special relationship with him. I see now, however, that the same law of causation has brought about your relationship with him."

"But only through you."

"That may be true, but on a deeper level, you already knew him."

"On a deeper level?"

"Yes, through what we call oneness with Buddha." Monk Dasol mentioned this only in passing, but it left the vague impression that there was some destiny that had brought me together with Monk Dasol and Hyegang. Monk Dasol paused for a moment before going on. "Mrs. Kang, I would like to go to Cheongsol with you."

"To Cheongsol?"

"Yes."

I wondered what he was thinking. Why did he want to go to Cheongsol? I had no idea but imagined that there must be something between the colony of lepers and Hyegang.

"You could go. It's a little past Suwon on the train."

"Past Suwon?" Monk Dasol considered this. "If it's not too much trouble, I would appreciate it if you would go with me."

"You'd like for me to go, too?"

"Yes."

"If it's any help, I'll go."

"Thank you."

"How's this coming Sunday?"

"That would be fine."

"What time?"

"Why don't you choose a time that's convenient for you?"

"How's ten o'clock in the morning?"

"That's fine."

"Then would you like to meet at Seoul Station this Sunday, ten o'clock?"

"Yes."

We said goodbye, and I went back out into the street. It was swarming with people, and there was the belch of sticky heat. I walked slowly down the sidewalk among the people, the image of Monk Dasol swaying like rolling waves in my heart. I stopped and closed my eyes to still the image, which then began to grow until it had wrapped itself around my body.

I opened my eyes again and continued on my way. There was a clothing store not too far ahead, and wanting to buy a dress for Jaun, I went in.

Jaun ran out of the house when I rang the doorbell.

"Hi, Mom."

"Hi, Jaun. Have you eaten supper yet?"

"No, I've been waiting for you."

"You shouldn't have. You must be hungry."

"I'm all right." Then sadly she said, "Mom, Doug said he's leaving here tomorrow morning."

"Tomorrow morning?"

"Yes, he's already packed."

Doug came out of his room when he heard me come in. "You had a long day, Mrs. Kang."

"Yes, I did. I hear you're leaving tomorrow."

"That's right."

"Good for you."

"What do you mean 'good,' Mom?" Jaun asked, shaking my arm.

"I feel bad, too, but Doug needs to learn things and establish himself."

Dougienei muttered back at this. "Right, establishing himself? He'll be lucky if he doesn't end up established as a beggar on the street. These days, people are leaving farms to come to Seoul. Why does that cursed kid want to learn about farming?"

I looked at Doug. He looked embarrassed, but there was no longer any sign of resentment.

"Auntie, they teach farming even in universities," I said. "Why are you bothering your son so much? He's trying to live a right life."

"Live a right life? Can he live a right life when his stomach is rumbling from hunger?" Dougienei retorted.

I grew tired of the talk and went upstairs to my room. I had changed clothes and was washing up when Doug came upstairs. For a moment, he just stood there awkwardly.

"I'll be with you in a moment," I said. "Please have a seat."

"Thank you."

As I was coming out, drying my face with a towel, Doug asked an unexpected question. "Mrs. Kang, do you think a man like me could live for others?"

"What do you mean by living for others?" I asked after some thought.

"It's just a question," he answered quietly. He seemed to be embarrassed by his assumption that he, who had not even graduated from high school, could live for others.

I took the question seriously. "Of course, you can."

It was clear that Doug had been thinking about this for a long time and that he wanted my assurance that he was right in the conclusion he had arrived at.

"Doug, suppose we are building a house. Now, to build a house, you need many things. Not just the marble you put on the outside, but also the gravel and sand where you can't see it. To have a house, you need gravel and sand just as much as you need marble. No one can say that marble is more important than gravel and sand. They are all indispensable."

"But I'm wondering. Can someone like me be even like gravel and sand?"

"Of course. Surely, you'll do it beautifully."

"Thank you, Mrs. Kang. I needed to hear that from you."

"Do your best, no matter how difficult it might seem."

"I will."

"And show your mother some affection."

"That's a problem for me. How can a man who doesn't love his mother be of service to others?"

"You can serve others, even though it's not right not to love your mother."

"No, it's not right," he agreed.

"Someday, you'll come to feel affection for your mother. It's something that comes as you grow older."

Doug said nothing more and left the room. Once more, I felt grateful for his will to live a meaningful life. I prayed he would bring forth much fruit.

No sooner had Doug gone out when Jaun came in. "This dress is very pretty, Mom."

"Do you like it?"

"Very much. It looks Dutch, doesn't it?"

"Right, except it doesn't have an apron."

"You should have bought this for me before."

"Before?"

"Yes, I could have worn it last Sunday."

It was apparent Jaun had thought of Hyegang first when she saw the dress. I smiled, thinking how Jaun was growing up so fast.

"I have some things to do right now. Will you go to bed, Jaun?"

"You go ahead, Mom. I'll read a little before going to sleep." Jaun went to her room, holding the Dutch dress before her.

It was agonizing to see Hyegang. He seemed to be deteriorating by the day. There were some days that would pass without him speaking one word. His face, which had always been calm and clear, was now almost transparent in its purity. Spiritually, too, he was in the process of filtering out impurities.

Watching this transformation was heartrending. Whether or not this was some preparation for his leap to a higher spiritual awareness, it was hard not to think this was cruel. Hyegang was a boy, only seventeen years old. Other boys his age were growing innocently, sometimes scolded, sometimes praised. But destiny had dictated that this was not to be for Hyegang. Witnessing his turmoil brought to mind what comfort lay in the ordinary destiny of others.

Hyegang was a boy who had been catapulted far away from ordinary existence to float alone in the empty sky. Nothing was real to him. In this state, only his studies helped to provide some rhythm in his life. Accordingly, he poured all his energies into them.

Even Mrs. Hahn, who was always saying she'd lost interest in teaching such underachieving students, had nothing but praise for Hyegang. "Hyegang's English is excellent," she would say. "His pronunciation needs some work, but his ability for comprehension is superb."

This dissonance was indicative of Hyegang's life and, at some level, represented the cause of his loneliness. He had no friends. His classmates, partly out of envy and partly out of respect, kept their distance. Outwardly, Hyegang seemed undisturbed by this, but the pain of his loneliness must have been incredible.

After closing session one day, I'd come back to the staff room and was sitting at my desk, letting fatigue course through my weak body. July's sticky heat added to my physical and mental exhaustion.

"Do you know what today's discomfort index is?" It was Mrs. Hahn's voice.

"I heard it's eighty-six," answered the geography teacher.

"So that's why I feel so terrible."

The conversation made me smile. It was interesting to think that modern science had devised a way to take humidity and temperature to measure discomfort. It was even more interesting to think that people would accept this measure so uncritically.

"It's too hot in Korea during the summer," Mrs. Hahn said.

"I agree. This is too hot."

"Summer in Los Angeles is like early autumn here."

"Is that right?"

"Yes. We would wear a light jacket all year round."

"It must be nice."

"It is. The weekends start on Friday afternoon, and every weekend people leave the city for vacation."

"Why didn't you stay there?"

"We could have if we'd applied for an extension on Daddy's project, but instead, we just came back."

"Does your husband still go into the field for his research?"

"Quite often. By the way, Daddy will be on TV tonight."

Listening to this exchange between Mrs. Hahn and the geography teacher, the fine arts teacher muttered quietly, "Daddy? Is he her daddy? Daddy, Daddy—she's bragging about him all the time."

"Happy people tend to want to express their happiness for others, don't they?" I said.

"Happiness? No, it's idleness. They're idle, like water collected in a bog."

"People are happy when they're idle."

"If they're factory workers or shopkeepers, yes. But her husband is a scholar. A university professor should always be striving for greatness."

"Who knows? Maybe he'll achieve it."

"How could he, going go-go dancing all the time with the kids and trying to satisfy his senses?"

"You seem to know a lot about Mrs. Hahn's husband. How did you learn all this?"

"Do you think I know all this because I want to? No! Only because she's always bragging about her Daddy and I can't not hear it, even with my ears plugged with cotton balls."

He was right. Nobody liked to listen to Mrs. Hahn, some going as far as sticking cotton in their ears.

"Do you remember a phrase that goes, 'a knight riding on a white horse'?" I asked the fine arts teacher.

"Yes, 'Wilderness,' isn't it?"

"That might be right."

"What made you think of it?"

"Don't you think a knight riding on a white horse would look nice?"

"I suppose he might."

"I'd like to find a nice man I could fall completely in love with."

The fine arts teacher laughed loudly. "You sound like a young girl."

"Sorry, I'm an old young girl." I smiled at him and got up to leave. Mrs. Hahn's trivial chatter was making the hot summer afternoon even more unbearable.

The trees in the schoolyard drooped under the fierce heat of the sun. What a miserable fate, to be a tree standing all day in this blistering heat, I thought. It's been said, "Life is suffering." Did this refer to these miserable trees?

After washing at the water tap, I was on my way back into the school when I spotted Hyegang sitting under the maidenhair tree. At first, I tried to pretend I hadn't seen him and went on my way, but then, changing my mind, I went to where he was sitting. Hyegang was watching something on the ground.

"What are you doing, Hyegang?" I asked casually.

Hyegang started at my voice and looked up. His face brightened.

"Mrs. Kang, have a seat here. Please." He moved to one end of the bench to make room for me.

"What were you looking at?"

"I was watching an earthworm."

"An earthworm?"

"Yes." Hyegang nodded toward the worm. Dried almost to a shrivel, it was writhing under the afternoon sun. It seemed to me a silent, horrifying cry for life.

"Why are you looking at this worm?"

"I was thinking, will this worm be born again as a worm in its next life?"

"Maybe, if you believe in reincarnation."

"Monk Dasol once told me about a cow that grazed next to a temple. It was freed from its animal existence in its next life because it had heard the monks reciting their scriptures every day."

"If that's true, you're on your way to a better life, aren't you, Hyegang?"

"I've grown up all my life listening to their sutras."

"That's a great privilege."

"I think so, too."

I had mixed feelings about this. That he was struggling to affirm his life was clear to me. I turned blankly to the parched ground, where the worm was still in its death struggle. After some time, Hyegang stood up and went to the water tap, returning with a plastic dipper full of water. He emptied the dipper on the ground under the maidenhair tree. Then he picked up the worm with twigs and buried it in the moistened soil.

"I believe this worm will at least be born a smarter worm in its next life," he said.

"Why do you think that?"

"Because it was buried by the hand of a boy who grew up listening to the scriptures." Hyegang grinned.

Sunday morning broke bright and clear, white clouds floating high in the blue sky. The clouds reminded me that I had to meet Monk Dasol. I hurried to clean the house, which was not a problem since there was really no one to make the house messy. But each week, there was some dust gathered in the cracks and corners of the rooms. I did the dusting on Sundays, even though Dougienei was in charge of housekeeping duties. It was too much to expect for her to do every little bit.

I tied a bandanna around my head and began dusting the tops of the books in the study. There is an old saying: "You are hardly aware of when someone is there, but you are keenly aware when someone is gone." I felt that now. I had barely noticed when Doug was with us, but now that he was gone, the house seemed completely vacant.

After going over the house, I went to wash. Even in the hot summer, the cold water on my body was startling, but it left me feeling cool and refreshed afterwards. The sensation was incomparable to anything else in the world.

Jaun left for my sister's house after breakfast. She was smiling, happy to be visiting her aunt, whom she had not seen for some time.

I selected a blue-and-white dress and placed a matching sunhat in my bag. With a light heart, I boarded the bus for Seoul Station. The station was crawling with people as usual, but cutting through the crowd, I quickly spotted Monk Dasol standing in front of the waiting room. I nearly ran to him.

"How are you, Monk Dasol?" I said in greeting, and he responded with a bright smile.

When I turned to buy the tickets, he showed me the two he had already bought. Cheongsol was printed on them in big black letters. They brought to mind a vague impression of two people coming together to one point.

We took our place in line and, after showing our tickets, were ushered through the gates. There was a maze of going up and down stairs to the platform, but soon we were on the train and taking our seats. I took care to sit a proper distance from Monk Dasol so as not to sit on his robe. The train lurched forward, moved slowly, and then we were on our way.

"They say life is a journey," Monk Dasol said.

"Yes, I've heard that, too, in a pop song," I answered, smiling.

"That's right. It was in a pop song."

"You listen to pop?"

"I do. And I like it, too."

"You like pop songs?"

"Yes, quite," Monk revealed without hesitation.

"It's funny that a monk would like pop songs."

"I don't see why. We look like ordinary people, so why shouldn't we feel the same?"

I looked at him for a moment before breaking out into laughter. He was so free from pretense. It was a refreshing change.

The train continued on, joggling over the Han River Bridge and through Yeongdeungpo on its way to Suwon. Fields and green hills appeared now and then between the tall smokestacks and high-rises. Everything looked bleached under the white-hot sun.

Monk Dasol and I talked easily, as we watched the landscape whir by and the train gently jostled us back and forth. It was as if we had known each other a long time.

"Cheongsol is next," I said.

"Then we should get ready," Monk Dasol replied.

"There's nothing to get ready. We don't have any baggage."

"Aren't our bodies baggage, in a way?"

Yes, baggage, a burden we must carry around until we die. This baggage of desires—it eats, sleeps, and feels. If we did not have it, could our souls be free?

"Monk Dasol, have you heard of negative lepers?"

"A leprosy patient, when he or she is completely cured, is called a negative patient."

"Does this mean they are no longer contagious?"

"That's right. Some carry the germ, but they're not contagious."

"Can they have children?"

"Lepers can't have children, but negative lepers, I believe, are able to."

"Children born to lepers are born to a particular fate."

"I think so."

"How do you come by your fate?"

"I don't know, except that it has to do with the law of causation."

This made me smile. "This man is honest," I thought to myself, recalling how I'd felt before.

"Providence can be cruel. Why did it confer passion on people and allow them to produce fruit?"

"It is the cruelest of all truths that people are passionate. The vicious cycle of birth and death can be said to be rooted in passion."

"The basic cause of birth and death is passion?"

"That's right? The life of an ordinary mortal revolves around passions. The process of removing these passions makes one a bodhisattva. To have completely removed them from life, that is to have achieved the Buddhahood, or enlightenment."

"How about monks?"

"Those who practice the Way are in the process of trying to uproot their passions."

"It seems that for those practicing the Way, passion is the greatest obstacle."

"It is the greatest obstacle. Buddha himself once said, 'If there were one more terrible thing like passion, no one would dare venture to embark upon the path of truth.'"

I gazed at Monk Dasol's gray sacred robe. Where was this monk going, that he must subdue that fierceness which finds its source in him?

The train pulled up to Cheongsol Station. Because it was a small station, there were not many passengers boarding or getting off. Monk Dasol and I gave our tickets to the conductor, who looked at us sideways. We must have made an unusual pair.

"You would like to go to the hamlet?" I asked.

"Yes."

"Then we should go this way."

I led Monk Dasol out of the town and down the river bank. Rice in the paddies grew a dark, rich green. The smell of these plants and the earth, even mingled in the humid air, was sweet. I inhaled deeply, wanting to take it all in. I took the hat out of my bag and put it on. When I did, Monk Dasol looked at me, his face flushed.

The singing of the frogs in the fields surrounded us, making me smile. The sound reminded me of noisy young women. At times, a stork floated overhead, its white wings stretched, sometimes dipping down toward the fields. Their white bodies, supported on long legs, contrasted sharply against the dark-green background.

"What are you going to do once we get to the hamlet?" I asked.

"Do? I just wanted to see." His face was solemn. He'd used the word "just," but he couldn't have come all this way for nothing. What had brought him?

As I watched Monk Dasol's black shoes ahead of me on the path, I was reminded of something he'd once said: "The most important thing is to practice. You can know things theoretically, but until you put them into practice, what good are they?" The remark resonated in my heart.

A distance down the path, a small hut came into view. Its roof was made of galvanized steel, and we could see inside, where there was a small room and a kitchen. The hut appeared to be deserted, the way the paper on the doors and windows were all tattered and torn out. There was a small wooden stoop that led out from the front door, well worn.

I hadn't noticed the hut when I was here last; why do I see it now?

Both sides of the creek were lined with wild rose bushes that grew thick. I remembered how, as a small girl, I used to play in fields like this. That had been thirty years ago.

We walked slowly but, before long, arrived at the old wooden bridge. It lay as it did before: black and decayed, gaps where the planks had rotted off.

"The hamlet is right across this bridge," I said.

"I see." Monk Dasol looked at the bridge for a moment, then looked beyond it at the hills in the distance. In the water below, there were sand and pebbles, schools of minnows, and white clouds, reflected from the sky above.

"Will you go across with me, Mrs. Kang?"

"Yes, I will."

"Then, let's go. Be careful." He stepped onto the narrow bridge ahead of me. Once, halfway across, he turned around to see how I was doing, a look of concern on his face.

Past the bridge, the path sloped slightly uphill into the village. Nestled in a thick forest of pines that spread up the hill behind it, the village was made up of about ten huts, which stood like stables in a row. It was obvious that we were strangers in this cozy setting. The thought made us tense. There was a lone woman drawing water from a well nearby, and as we passed into the village, she gazed at us vacantly. Her face was deformed, her nose sunk and her eyebrows gone. Her hand, which was now holding onto a vessel of water, was missing two fingers.

Monk Dasol looked at the woman in silence before speaking. "Excuse me, but would you mind it if we visited?"

The woman gave us one more look but said nothing before placing the vessel atop her head and walking swiftly away. Monk Dasol and I turned to each other.

"It doesn't look like they're very welcome to visitors here," I said.

"No, it certainly doesn't."

We walked further into the village but were soon approached by a group of men, suspicion and hostility in their eyes.

"Excuse us," Monk Dasol said. "We were just passing by." Monk Dasol put the palms of his hands together and bowed.

"Where are you from?" asked one of them.

"We are from a Buddhist temple not far from here."

"This place is not for people."

"Not for people?" Monk Dasol smiled gently.

Another man, this one looking younger than the others, spoke. "As you can see…" He looked annoyed that he would have to explain and left the sentence hanging. "This is not for you to visit. Please go back to where you came from."

"Being that we're here, won't you allow us a few minutes before we do?" Monk Dasol asked politely.

"If you're looking for donations, you're looking in the wrong village," the young man said, and turned to walk away.

Before anything else could happen, a woman came out of the hut, wiping sweat from her brow. "She's gone," she cried. "She's gone at last."

"Gone? That's good. Good for her," an old man murmured.

"A woman has passed away. Go, now," the young man said to us.

The woman who had announced the death now seemed to notice us for the first time. "Who is this master?" she asked.

"It doesn't matter who he is," the young man answered bitterly.

"Please, Master, won't you come in and pray for the dead?" the woman asked, pulling on Monk Dasol's sleeve with deformed hands. Monk Dasol turned to the men in deference.

"What marvelous luck!" the woman said in a southern accent. "Masters won't come here even when we ask. Now here is one who has come on his own." She motioned to the men. "Well, don't just stand there. Let's go in."

"Would you like me to go in also?" Monk Dasol asked the men.

The woman tugged at his sleeve impatiently. "Why are you so slow? You don't have to ask them. Won't you just come in. Pray that she may go on to a better place in her next life."

"Then I'll pray for her." Monk Dasol ducked into the hut. After some hesitation, I followed, lifting the straw mat that hung in the doorway. Inside, the room was empty except for the dark gloom that infested it and the body of the dead woman.

"Would you go out and wait for a few minutes?" the young man said. The men had joined us in the hut. "We would like to cover the sores on her face."

While Monk Dasol and I waited outside on the stoop, we exchanged smiles. The young man soon came out to tell us we could go back in.

A thin black sheet had been laid over the corpse, but the foul stench still hung in the air. Monk Dasol sat cross-legged beside the covered body. People gathered around and, with tearful faces, looked on.

"Who is the master?" one asked.

"They say he came on his own."

"At least the old woman is lucky in death."

"You're right. What a blessing it is to pass into the other world while listening to a master reading the scriptures."

"To die listening to the scriptures—how could people like us expect this privilege?"

I felt a pang in my heart as I listened. It was obvious that life was precious to them even as they wished to go to a better place in the afterlife.

Monk Dasol began his recitation of the *Heart Sutra*:

> Avalokiteśvara, the Holy Lord and Bodhisattva, was moving in the deep course of the Wisdom which goes beyond. He looked down from on high; he beheld but five heaps and he saw that in their own-being they were empty.

> Here, O Sariputra, form is emptiness and the very emptiness is form, emptiness does not differ from form, form does not differ from emptiness; whatever is form, that is emptiness; whatever is emptiness, that is form; the same is true of feelings, perceptions, impulses, and consciousness.

> Here, O Sariputra, all dharmas are marked with emptiness; they are not produced or stopped, not defiled or immaculate, not deficient or complete.

> Therefore, O Sariputra, in emptiness,
> there is neither form nor feeling—

Monk Dasol recited the scriptures in an even and calm voice. His eyes were closed gently. The men and women who had gathered around now wept quietly. They wiped away tears with deformed hands. I felt tears running down my own cheeks.

The crying had grown to a wail by the time Monk Dasol finished his recitation, and now many were pounding the ground in mournful anguish. It was as if somehow the focus of their lament had turned from the death of the old woman to the misery of their own lives. The stench in the small dark room was becoming unbearable.

"Everybody, quit it." The young man was dry-eyed and contemptuous.

"Master, thank you so much," said the woman. "How can we ever repay you?" Her hands were clasped together as she bowed deeply. The gesture stirred others to speak.

"Yes, how kind of him to pray for miserable beings like us on such a hot day," they said.

Monk Dasol replied in a gentle voice, "It is of much greater use to listen to the scriptures while one is still alive than it is to listen to them after death. By reciting the scriptures with diligence, you may eradicate the layers of bad karma accumulated about you."

"We know that, but how can we listen to the scriptures if we can't attend a temple?" asked a woman. Her face was deformed almost beyond recognition.

"Bring me a pail of water with a gourd dipper upside down in it," said Monk Dasol.

A woman stood up swiftly and came back with a big pail of water, a gourd upside down in it. Monk Dasol held the dipper with one hand and struck it with the other, in the way one would strike a bell. He asked the people to repeat after him.

"Gwanseeum Bosal, Gwanseeum Bosal." He repeated again and again the name of the Bodhisattva the Compassionate. The woman who had pleaded with Monk Dasol to pray now was the first to join the recitation. Others began to follow, at first shyly but then louder and louder. Soon the room was filled with spiritual intensity, and the chanting became like singing, mournful singing.

When Monk Dasol left the room afterwards, the people followed him.

"Master, where is your temple?" the young man asked.

"Not far from here."

"Will you come again?" asked the woman.

"I will."

"When?" she asked. "I'll expect your return."

"When is it good for you?"

"We rest on the first and third Sunday of every month," the young man offered. "On other days, we are working in the marketplace."

"I'll come on the third Sunday of every month," said Monk Dasol.

"Oh, Master, what a great favor to us!"

"Please don't call me master. I'm a monk." Monk Dasol smiled gently and clasped his hands before them. The people clasped their hands in return and bowed. At that, we turned to leave the village.

"Namu Gwanseeum Bosal," said Monk Dasol, calling the name of the Bodhisattva the Compassionate in a sigh.

The sun beat down on us with all its intensity. Under its glare, Monk Dasol pointed to the creek as we came to it. "Should we go down and wash our hands there?"

We went to the creek and dipped our hands in the cool water, looking down at our hands in silence.

"Will you come again?" he asked.

"If you wish."

"I do."

We smiled at our reflections in the water.

CHAPTER SEVEN:
July (II)

With the final examinations now over, the teachers were busy compiling grades in their reports, which they were required to do before submitting these reports to each student's homeroom teacher. The homeroom teachers were then to total up the students' marks, calculate their average grades, and determine their standing in the class.

"It's awfully hot in here," the music teacher complained, staring at the electric fan, which now turned drowsily. "I'd better hurry up, so then I can go home where it's air-conditioned."

The other teachers, who were now wrestling with grade sheets and calculators, looked up curiously. The music teacher was not in charge of any class, so was excused from the trouble of calculating grades. It was pure rudeness on her part to gabble on while the other teachers labored on in silence.

"Mrs. Lee, please don't provoke us," the geography teacher said. "Who knows, maybe one of us will someday dig up a gold nugget with our sweet potatoes, too." The other teachers laughed in support.

"What's the matter with you all?" the music teacher whined. "It's no business of yours how I use my money."

"That's right." The geography teacher continued with his sarcasm. "What else is money good for?" The reference to her money had obviously touched a nerve in him.

According to Mrs. Hahn, the music teacher had come by her money from a sweet potato farm her parents-in-law had owned in the Yeongdong area. The property had been under the control of the Japanese, but after liberation, it was passed to her parents-in-law, who had been working there for them. Combined with the skyrocketing land prices of the time, this made them overnight millionaires. The couple died soon afterwards, however, and the music teacher benefited.

The implication, as Mrs. Hahn made clear in her story, was that there was nothing at all good about the music teacher's wealth. The geography teacher and the fine arts teacher shared the same feeling of disgust.

"The geography teacher has a sweet potato garden," the fine arts teacher said now. "Maybe he'll strike gold in it. But I don't have a garden. Where is my hope?"

"I'll tell you," answered the music teacher. "Your hope is in your mouth."

"My mouth?"

"Yes, we're in the business of selling words. So where else can we find our hope except in the source of our words?"

Chapter Seven: July (II)

"The business of selling words? There's not much capital investment required for that, is there?"

"I see now," the music teacher chimed in, wiping her mouth with the back of her hand. "My mouth is a treasure. As long as I carry this around in my face, I can eat three times a day." The other teachers laughed appreciatively.

The music teacher's reference to her air-conditioned home highlighted the sad truth that our mouths were all we had.

"In ten years of teaching, I've never seen a student earn one hundred percent in my class. But Hyegang has done it," the physics teacher said as he handed his grade sheet to me.

"He got a perfect score in my class, too," said Mrs. Hahn.

"Good heavens, he got one in math, too."

The geography teacher and the German language teacher reported that Hyegang had achieved the same in their classes.

"If that's the case, I have no choice but to give him a sixty percent in physical education."

"Then you are a failure as a teacher."

"Why is that?"

"While all the other teachers were able to teach him perfectly, you were only able to teach him sixty percent."

The phys. ed. teacher laughed sheepishly at this. "Then he gets one hundred percent in my class, too."

"Well, I'm giving him a ninety," the music teacher said. Her marks were strictly performance-based.

"Congratulations, Mrs. Kang. This reflects well on you as a homeroom teacher." The other teachers joked pleasantly as they submitted their grade reports. Hyegang's mark in music had dropped his grade to 99.4 percent, but this was the highest recorded in the school's history.

"Mrs. Kang, you mustn't tell Hyegang about this," said the dean of students.

"Why not?"

"Remember? He hates to be called the first."

"That's right. You can't tell him. He might refuse to accept the watch." Each year, the founder of the school presented a watch to the student with the highest mark. We laughed at the suggestion.

I went to the library after finishing with the grade sheets. The library was the quietest and coolest room in the school, so this was a frequent hideout for me each summer. The librarian greeted me with her usual cheerful smile.

"Don't you get sleepy sitting alone like this all day long?" I asked.

"Of course, I do. As a matter of fact, I was dozing off just now," she said with a laugh.

I sat at the table as the librarian pushed a pile of papers toward me. They were mostly academic papers and newsletters. I would skim through them whenever I was here.

"There's a lot this time," I said. After flipping through several, I came to one titled "The Religious World." A few pages into it was an announcement: "You are cordially invited to a seminar to be held with the topic, 'The Social

Role of Religion.' The panel will include the following representatives:

Protestant	Pastor K.
Buddhism	Monk Dasol
Catholic	Priest J.
Chondogyo	Leader H."

I was pleasantly surprised to come across Monk Dasol's name like this. The announcement went on to say that the seminar began at five thirty that afternoon. If I hurried, I could make it. There was a brief moment of hesitation, but then I made up my mind to attend. It would be interesting to hear, first of all, what Monk Dasol had to say and also the views of these other religious leaders.

It looked like it was about to rain when I left the library. The air was even heavier and hotter than usual, and the flies were everywhere.

I returned to the staff room and prepared to leave. As I was looking up at the clock one more time, the fine arts teacher asked, "You have somewhere to go, Mrs. Kang?"

"Yes."

"Where?"

"An interesting place."

"The movies?"

"No, a seminar I want to attend."

"Sounds informative."

"Why don't you come with me?"

"Sorry, I'm busy. But I want to hear what you've learned later." He looked up at the clock. "Well, time to go."

The sun was still high in the sky when I left the school. Wanting to arrive in time, I hailed a taxi.

There was already a large crowd waiting to enter the auditorium when I arrived at the Press Center. But the speakers had not arrived, as early as it was. I took one of the programs that were being handed at the entrance and, taking a seat in the rear, browsed through it.

The speakers took their places on the stage about five minutes before the seminar was scheduled to begin. I watched them but was careful not to catch Monk Dasol's gaze. Once seated, Monk Dasol closed his eyes lightly and clasped his hands before him, as he had done after the lecture at the temple. A clear aura was almost visible around him.

After a few introductory remarks by the man presiding over the seminar, Pastor K. of the Protestant Church came up to the podium and spoke about social participation from the standpoint of Christians. During his talk, I glanced at Monk Dasol from time to time. His expression remained unchanged.

Following Pastor K., Monk Dasol approached the lectern. He clasped his hands and bowed to the audience before taking his place at the microphone. His talk began with a historical overview of the role played in society by Buddhism since its introduction to Korea, detailing how certain monks had contributed significantly through different periods of the nation's history. He concluded by saying that although in Buddhism one aims to attain the Buddhahood through self-fulfillment, one does not strive to achieve self-fulfillment in itself but cherishes an earnest wish to help others attain the Buddhahood; thus Buddhists fundamentally concern themselves with society.

As I watched Monk Dasol draw on his broad and deep knowledge and speak with so much authority, I remembered our meeting the previous Sunday. He had mentioned his fondness for pop songs and talked about the struggles he had with his inner passions. He had, with clasped hands, bowed to a leper and struck a gourd dipper in prayer for the dead. Which of these represented this monk? It seemed to me that they all did, and yet at the same time, none of them did.

Part of the *Heart Sutra* reads "neither defiled nor immaculate." Some interpret this to refer to true emptiness, where everything is empty of its own being and therefore free of defilement or immaculacy. Had Monk Dasol achieved this state?

Priest J. of the Catholic Church and Leader H. of the Chondogyo took their turns respectively after Monk Dasol. The underlying theme of these speakers, it seemed to me, was the supreme importance of love and service.

Love and service, the most fundamental and pure of all truths. Nobody, except a few sages, have been able to practice them perfectly.

To love unconditionally seemed too lofty an ideal. I was dwarfed by comparison; no matter how hard I might stretch out my arm, I could never reach it. At this thought, Monk Dasol's words returned to me: "The most important thing is to practice. You can know things theoretically, but until you put them into practice, what good are they?"

It was raining hard in the streets when I left the auditorium following the speeches and discussions. People huddled in the entrance. Some had come with umbrellas, and they disappeared triumphantly into the dark, while we looked on at the great streaks of rain. Someone behind me spoke. "Would you like to share this umbrella with me?" It was Monk Dasol's voice. I turned around, embarrassed to have been found out.

"Which way are you going, Mrs. Kang?"

"Toward Gwanghwamun."

"Let's go that way then. I can catch a bus there, too."

Monk Dasol opened the umbrella and we walked under it. I could feel his warmth as my arm brushed against his.

"It was a bright afternoon. How did you know to bring an umbrella?"

"For an unmarried person like me, the most troublesome thing in life is to get wet. So I take an umbrella when it looks even slightly like rain."

"I didn't want you to see me, but I guess the rain caught me."

"It wasn't the rain. I saw you right away."

"I read about the seminar in the paper and thought it would be interesting to attend," I said, fumbling for an excuse to have been there.

"What's so interesting about it? It was nonsense, like empty cans clattering on the arms of a scarecrow."

"I learned many things today."

"Only what has been said before by ancient sages. Intellectuals today are only repeating what they've stolen from sages who lived thousands of years ago."

"Stolen?"

"Did I use too strong a word? Maybe. But that's what I've always thought."

"No, you're right. And I'm really someone who steals from intellectuals."

"So now we're both thieves." He laughed pleasantly. It was not the first time I'd heard him laugh, but this time it was so honest and forthright, it cheered me.

"You catch the bus on this side of street, don't you?" I asked.

"Yes."

"Then I'd better say goodbye here." I bowed.

"Let me walk you to your bus stop."

"No, you don't have to. It's already too late."

"But I'd appear rude if I didn't, wouldn't I?" Monk Dasol smiled playfully.

We took the passage that went under the street and arrived at my bus stop.

"See you at Seoul Station this Sunday, ten o'clock," I reminded him.

"I'll remember."

"Goodbye, Monk Dasol."

I boarded the bus and, through the window, watched him walk slowly away. From behind, his figure looked even more immersed in quietude. It was hard to imagine that he'd cracked a joke just a few minutes before. I felt the mystery of this man.

On Saturday evening, I went with Jaun to my younger sister's house. My brother-in-law's job in the foreign trade business often took him on overseas business trips, leaving my sister and her son alone at home much of the time. My sister greeted us at the gate, a big smile on her face and her hands covered with clay.

"What's all that clay over your hands?" I asked.

"Oh, this? Come in, I want to show you something." She led us onto the hardwood floor of her living room. There was a small pottery wheel, and on a large square table beside it was a lump of clay covered in plastic.

"You've become interested in pottery?"

"Yes. I'm bored."

"You're so lucky to be making pottery in an air-conditioned house."

"Lucky?" she guffawed. "Don't make me laugh. I wish I could just run away."

"You're talking like when you were a little girl."

"That's what drives me so crazy. If I were still young, I'd have run away a long time ago." She lay the vinyl tarp over the spun pots and went to the bathroom to wash her hands.

I took a look around the house. It had been a while since I'd visited. There were many new pieces of furniture and antiques that hadn't been there on my last visit. "Good heavens, you buy a lot these days," I said.

"It's your brother-in-law's fault. He buys these things just because someone says it's good."

"You graduated from an art college. Don't you have any input?"

"What's the use? I try to talk to him about the beauty of empty space, but it's like reciting the scriptures to an ox. He thinks the more expensive pieces around, the better. What can I do?"

"He has unique tastes, doesn't he?"

"Yes, he certainly is unique. When we were dating, he would pretend to have these refined tastes. He was always talking about aesthetics and stuff like that."

"So, he's developed his vulgarity from living with you?"

"No, it's the other way around. I've become vulgar from living with him."

"Maybe he makes too much money, and that's why price is everything to him."

"You're probably right. He's at his best where money is concerned."

I laughed at the remark.

"Kihae, I'm bored," she continued. "It's too simple to live when everything comes with a push of a button."

"Your life is too easy," I said. "That's why you're talking like this. Remember there are many people out there who can't afford nearly what you have, even though they work their fingers to the bone."

"I'd rather be them sometimes. At least, their lives are real."

"Your life isn't real?"

"I feel like a corpse. A living corpse."

"That's gross. Why do you talk like that?"

"Because it's true."

"You're making no sense. You have everything you could possibly want to be happy."

"No, it's all illusion. While you're working to get it, it means everything, but once you have it, it's nothing."

"I wouldn't know."

"I envy you. You do things for a reason."

"I do things to feed myself," I said. I was not familiar with abstract terms like happiness. "Why don't you find something to do that's meaningful?"

"How do I do that?"

"I can't tell you because it's different for different people. What's most valuable to you? Maybe that's what's meaningful to you."

"Valuable things?"

"Well," I said, not liking that term either. "Something like that."

"They don't interest me." My sister's bluntness dazed me slightly.

"What interests you then?"

"I don't know. Maybe nothing interests me."

"Your husband isn't why you're unhappy. You're unhappy because of yourself."

"He's too crude anyway."

"You're the one in trouble here, it seems. You're neither refined nor crude." I drove in almost cruelly on my sister.

A pond in the backyard, a beautiful house, full furnishings, antiques everywhere, an inelegant but family-oriented husband, a healthy son—she had too much. It was more than any human being deserved to have in this world.

To people working so that they may eat three times a day, my sister's life was probably like heaven. When we think of heaven, we tend to think of abundance, where nothing is lacking. But my sister's situation proved to me that abundance in heaven was surely not in material things.

"I'm thirsty," I said. "Can I have something to drink?"

"Oh, where are my manners? By the way, where's Jaun?" My sister pushed a button on the intercom and spoke into it. "Bring something to drink."

After few minutes, a maid with long hair brought in a tray. On it were bottles of orange juice imported from the U.S., artfully peeled melons, and cookies.

"Jaun, help yourself, okay?" my sister said.

Jaun nodded and took some of the cookies. She was unusually quiet, though I couldn't tell if it was because of the intimidating luxury of the house or because she was not familiar with her aunt.

"Jaun, if you're finished with your juice, you can go outside and play," I said.

"Thank you." Liberated, Jaun jumped up and bounded out.

"Where's your husband?"

"I don't know. Somewhere in Europe probably."

I tried another subject. "Have you been doing this pottery long?"

"About two months."

"Dedicate yourself to it, and you could become a first-class artist."

"What would be the point? No, I'm just doing this to pass time."

"How about religion? Have you thought of that? Buddhism, Catholicism, or something."

"I don't understand you, Kihae. Do you really believe in that stuff?"

"Yes."

"You mean, you actually believe in the Buddha, God, or whatever?"

"Of course."

"What an anachronism! How can you believe in that stuff in this time and age?"

"Now I know why you're so unhappy. It's because you're so impudent. You only believe in the superficial and say you like nothing."

"You talk like a clergyman. I'm not interested."

"That's all right. I won't talk about it anymore."

I took a sip of the orange juice and leaned back in the sofa, thinking, "If your husband was not in the business of making money and if he wasn't so vulgar, you would be far more miserable than you are now."

If anything, it is suffering that makes the soul sublime. Without first going through dark times, a person cannot elevate to a higher plane. It seemed to me that the reason why Hyegang and Doug were so pure in their hearts was that they knew what it was to suffer. God confers trying times only upon the chosen.

"Kihae, let's sit on the floor."

"That'd be fine with me."

The floor in the living room was inlaid with mother of pearl, and laid out on one side of the room was a thin futon, its covering made of purple silk.

"You can lie down there." My sister pointed to the futon.

"How about you?"

"I'll have another one spread out on this side." My sister pushed the button and spoke into it. Auntie Naju entered with a mattress.

"Hello, how are you?" she said when she saw me. Auntie Naju had been working in my sister's house for the past four or five years.

"I'm fine, thank you. And you?"

"Well, I am—" She left the room without finishing.

"She's been here a long time," I said.

"Yes, she's getting weak in the head, I think."

"Weak in the head? She looks better than you."

"Come on, Kihae, you're always putting me down like I'm still a child."

"I know, but you need to grow up. Life tastes better when you take it more seriously."

"There you go again. You've been teaching for so long, you even smell like a schoolmistress."

I didn't respond, wondering if it was true. I had been teaching for more than ten years, and it was a fear of mine that this had made me stale and trite. I smiled at the thought.

"I don't see Donghoon. Where is he?" I asked.

"He's at a violin lesson."

"Piano, and now violin?"

"Yes, both."

"Is he good?"

"Just all right."

"Poor boy, he's paying for having been born to the wrong mother."

This time, it was my sister who did not respond.

If wealth brings so much grief, why do you try so hard to get it? Wealth, power, and fame give happiness only in the right circumstances. But rarely are the circumstances right.

"This room is beyond cool," I went on. "It's cold in here."

"Sometimes, I put on an extra shirt."

"It's a different world."

"Not really. It's nothing special."

"Do you ever shop?"

"What for?"

"Not even for groceries?"

"All you have to do is phone, and they deliver it to you. Why would I want to go out there?"

"You might want to visit the marketplace just for something to do. You can watch the old ladies on the cement, trying to sell things not worth one hundred Won for the whole lot."

"Why would I want to see that?"

"Why? You can feel their pain, commiserate."

"Good heavens. You would have made a great wife to a pastor. Marrying a doctor, all you became was a widow. You are so cute."

"That's enough. What kind of person are you?"

My sister looked beyond the point of salvation. With the music teacher, there was some crudeness that gave grounds for some hope. But my sister was not crude enough. I remembered how the fine arts teacher had once joked, "If you're not good and you're not evil, you're beyond hope for salvation. The most unfortunate are those that can go neither to heaven or hell, but remain only in empty space." At least, the evil could be saved.

"This room is so cool, I'd like to take a nap. Can you give me a blanket?" I said.

My sister put out a beautifully embroidered quilt, and soon I was asleep.

"Kihae, wake up. It's dinnertime."

I woke at my sister's gentle urging. "What time is it?"

"A little past seven."

"Already? I must have been dead asleep."

"That reminds me of a dream I had last night."

"What kind of dream was that?"

"Mom was holding your hand and taking you to the mountains. You didn't want to go and kept looking back every so often, until I couldn't see you anymore. I came back home and Jaun was dressed all in white, and when she saw me, she came to me and cried in my arms. What a strange dream."

"Maybe it's an omen."

"No, it was just a dream."

"When I die, take good care of Jaun, will you?"

"Don't be silly, Kihae."

Jaun came in holding Donghoon's hand. "Mom, you slept so long."

"Maybe because it's so cool in here. Well, Donghoon, come to me. How have you been?"

Donghoon grinned and sat on my lap. He looked healthy and neat, like the son of a wealthy family should.

"Donghoon, didn't you miss your aunt?"

"I did."

"Then why didn't you visit?"

My sister said, "Last week, he was looking at an album, and when he came to a picture of you, he said, 'When I want to see Auntie, I can look at this picture.'"

"Oh no, you missed me that much?" Hearing this tugged at my heart. Donghoon had no grandmother, so an aunt was probably his dearest relative. "I should come see you more often." I put my cheek against Donghoon's.

"Let's go into the kitchen," my sister suggested.

The kitchen was as luxurious as the rest of the house. There were two large refrigerators standing side by side and an Italian-made teak table. Shiny silver platters, brimming with many kinds of food, were arranged on the table.

"It all looks so inviting," I said.

"You must be hungry. Go ahead. Jaun, you help yourself, too."

"How come Jaun is so much like a refined lady?" my sister added.

"Maybe because we're all alone."

"Kihae, try this. This is crab from Yeongdeok. It's world famous."

"Thanks. The food here is always delicious."

Tea and fruits followed dinner.

"Jaun, we should go," I said as we finished our tea.

"Why don't you stay over?"

"We have a home."

"Dougienei is there, isn't she?"

"I shouldn't."

"You don't have to work tomorrow, do you? Why don't you stay?" My sister was sad to see us leave. We'd had our differences over the years, but I was the only family she had.

"I should go," I said.

"How about you, Jaun? Would you like to stay here until tomorrow?"

Jaun looked at me for permission.

"You can play with Donghoon some more and come tomorrow, if you like," I said.

Jaun readily agreed to this. She had no brother of her own and was delighted at the prospect of spending more time with Donghoon.

"Jaun, I have to be somewhere tomorrow. Play with Donghoon, and then I'll phone you," I said, remembering that I was to meet with Monk Dasol tomorrow. I didn't want Jaun to come home only to find that I wasn't there.

"Don't worry. I'll have the driver take her home."

"Good. Have a good time. And remember, Donghoon, next time you'll visit our place, right?" I patted Donghoon on the cheek.

"Yes, Aunt. Goodbye." Donghoon bowed to me, also pleased that Jaun was staying the night.

I walked alone into the dark alleyway, where the day's humidity and heat lingered. The coolness of my sister's house was already a distant memory.

I woke a little late on Sunday, and still tired. Through the window beside my bed, I could see a wispy white cloud. A cool breeze flowed softly into the room. It was relaxing to lie and take this all in—relaxing to the mind as well as to the body. As I savored the morning from my bed, I thought of the leper colony. Was it the end of the world, or was it purgatory? I could not believe it to be of this world—that hamlet where people lived, waiting for Monk Dasol's return. Buddhism was foreign to them, yet they obviously believed in the Beyond and the salvation that could be found there. Maybe this was what religion was anyway. What was the point of memorizing scriptures and learning doctrines? Throwing ourselves humbly before a power, believing that power will watch over us in our times of suffering and despair—wasn't this religion?

I got out of bed to prepare for the trip. I showered, put on the blue-and-white dress, and put the hat in my bag.

"Auntie, would you mind cleaning in the corners this week?" I asked Dougienei.

"Not at all. Why? Are you going somewhere?"

"Yes, I have to leave now."

"Have a nice day."

On the way to the bus stop, I thought it might be good to buy some disinfectant and clothes for the villagers. I remembered the foul odor in the hut and the rags that the weeping old woman had been wearing. A drug store and a clothing store were nearby and had the things I was looking for.

Monk Dasol was waiting for me at Seoul Station.

"I'm late again," I said in way of apology.

"Well."

"I'll go and buy the tickets."

"I have them here." He was holding two tickets, Cheongsol printed on them in black.

"The law of causation seems to have an impact not only between people, but also between people and places," I said, smiling at Monk Dasol.

"It does seem so."

We went into the waiting room and lined up with the others, waiting to be admitted. After a short wait, we raced with the crowd onto the platform and boarded the train. The hectic pace gave me a boost.

"You can sit by the window," Monk Dasol offered.

"Thank you."

He waited until I'd taken my seat before sitting beside me. A cool breeze, from the open window and from the electric fan attached to the ceiling, moved over us. Before long, the train was making its way over the Han River Bridge.

"When is your vacation?" Monk Dasol asked as we looked out at the landscape scrolling by.

"It begins tomorrow."

"You must be looking forward to it."

"I am."

"How do you plan to spend it?"

"I'm hoping to get to some books I've been wanting to read. I've wanted to get to them for some time now, but it always goes nowhere. This time, I'm setting out a certain number of pages to read each day."

"Why do you want to read so diligently?"

"I try hard, but I'm still ignorant about so many things. Maybe I'm just a fool."

"It is good to be a fool. Buddha has said that it is our discriminating knowledge that is at the root of the vicious cycle of birth and death."

"Discriminating knowledge?"

"The ability to differentiate between right and wrong, good and bad."

"I've noticed that people who are quick to judge these things get tired very easily."

"Yes, they get tired."

"I'm a fool. But I'm quick to see these differences."

"That's terrible." Monk Dasol laughed.

"I'm serious."

"Your problem is no different than mine. That is why I'm laughing."

I could not help but laugh with him. "Last time, you said we were thieves. Now you're saying we're fools."

Monk Dasol looked out the window, his face now serene. The breeze that came in through the open window now seemed to be moving in my heart. In a rice paddy, farmers in straw hats sprayed insecticide with sprayers they carried under their arms. A white fog hovered over the field, and above it, birds flew.

Are those birds safe from the insecticide? Of all life in the heavens, on the earth, and in the seas, only man is isolated. He alone tries to invade and destroy.

Factories, houses, and other buildings stood here and there in the paddies and the fields. It was easy to see how mankind was eroding away at nature.

"Monk Dasol, where do you think human civilization is headed?"

"Somewhere, maybe."

"That doesn't make sense."

"East or west. If not, south or north."

"What?"

"Where else could it be headed?"

Was this a foolish answer to a foolish question? Or a profound answer to a foolish question?

We got off the train in Cheongsol. The ticket collector, seeming to recognize us, gave us the same sideways look he'd given us last time. We left the railway station in the direction of the creek.

The sun was fiercely hot as ever. I took the hat from my bag and put it on, glancing at Monk Dasol. He neither flushed nor moved away this time, but continued on his way, undisturbed. The rice in the paddies had turned dark green, and the green stretched endlessly away from us. Obviously, the sunshine and the water had done much for the rice plants. In the paddies, storks looked about for food. Their white bodies, couched in the green, struck me as fresh and pure.

We came to the log bridge, which lay across the clear stream darkly as before, like an old person waiting for death.

"After you."

"After you, Monk Dasol."

"I can't tell whether you came with me or I came with you," Monk Dasol joked. He was apologetic about having brought me here on such a hot summer day. I gave him a reassuring look.

Two small boys and a girl were playing in front of the hut as we approached. They looked to be seven or eight years old, perfectly healthy from all appearances. They stopped their game when they saw us approach.

"Where is everyone?" I asked, but even as I did, a voice sounded behind me.

"Oh! Master, you really came." It was the woman.

"Have you been well?" asked Monk Dasol.

"Well or not, I'm all right. But how thankful I am that you've come." She shifted in her place, apparently wanting to express her gratitude. "Could you wait here just a minute? I'll be right back."

Lifting the straw mat that hung in the doorway, she entered the hut, and after a few seconds, the young man emerged. It was clear he was the leader in this community.

"Oh, Master. Welcome." He greeted us with a wide smile. He'd warmed up to us ever since Monk Dasol's recitation of the scriptures.

Monk Dasol smiled in return and clasped his hands before him.

"It's too hot for you to have come all this way."

"I said I would come."

"Oh, words. You don't have to keep you word with miserable things like us."

Monk Dasol just smiled.

"I don't know what we should do," the young man went on. "You can see what conditions we live under. I don't dare ask you to come in. But you should sit somewhere." The young man's embarrassment was visible.

"We can go over there, to the pine trees." I pointed to the dense stand of trees behind the hut.

"That might be good. It's cool there."

We walked slowly toward the forest. The scent of pine overtook us.

"Here's a good place." With some effort, the young man carried two large flat stones, set them in the ground, and briskly brushed off the dirt. Parts of fingers were missing on his hands. "Please sit down."

"Thank you. Why don't you take a seat, Bosal-nim?" Monk Dasol said to me.

"Thank you." I sat on one of the stones the young man had prepared.

"How many households are there in this village?" Monk Dasol inquired.

"Fifteen. Oh yes, the old woman passed away. Fourteen."

"One person is one household?"

"Mostly. There are hardly any families. This cursed disease has separated us from our families."

"Then the families that are here are ones that formed here?"

"That's true, more or less. Even ones that are completely cured don't go home. They'd only be shunned there."

"But aren't their families waiting for them?" I asked.

"Our families wouldn't like us to go home. If we went back, they'd be separated from their community."

"I see." I could, for the first time, understand the nature of their sorrows, where to be alive was a sin. My heart filled with sympathy as I looked on their faces.

"That's why we get together and form villages like this." The young man spoke firmly. Even in his deformed face, I could see the determination there.

"So, many of you have families now?"

"We are human, and we need families."

"Are there some who live alone?"

"Yes, there were three, but one has died, so now there are two."

"Both old?"

"Yes, one is a woman in her seventies. As cursed as our lives are, they're stronger than hemp and won't be cut off easily."

"How do you make a living?"

"The old woman stays in her hut and never comes out. The other old woman is a peddler. The rest of us work at the hog farm."

"Do you earn enough from that?"

"Sometimes, it seems the hogs live better than we do."

"How about the old woman who doesn't work?"

"We give her spoonfuls of food from what we have."

"I see."

"The peddler does the best out of all of us. But who wants to go around showing that ugly face just to eat better? It's easier to spend the time with pigs." The young man, maybe because he was talking to a monk, spoke candidly and without reservation.

During a pause in the conversation, the woman who had greeted us earlier ran to us, waving her arms. "Why did you come all the way out here?"

"It's cool here. Why would they want to go into that stinking hut?" the young man replied.

The woman ignored the bluntness of his remark. "I told everyone the master was here. They were all surprised. They're coming this way now."

Indeed, there were people coming this way. Once they'd come near, however, they seemed at a loss what to do then. It must have been odd to have a visitor, let alone a monk in a holy robe.

"Oh, what are you standing there like poles for?" chided the woman. "Don't you remember? This is the master who did that great favor for us a couple weeks ago."

"How are you, Master?"

"Thank you for what you did last time."

"Thank you so much for not forgetting about us."

Their gratitude was heartfelt.

Monk Dasol stood up and extended his hands. "How have you been? Please take a seat."

"The master has come to us in this hot weather. Have a seat and listen to his words," the young man said, and the others obeyed.

"Thank you for coming. I also give thanks to the special relationship we had in Buddha in our previous lives for bringing us together like this." With this introduction, Monk Dasol went on to explain the concepts of karma, reincarnation, and the law of causation, using understandable terms. He remarked that just as our previous karma determined our present situation, leading a wholesome life in this world will bless us in our next life.

It was indeed an unusual type of Buddhist service. These souls that had suffered so terribly as they watched their bodies rot—were they now to have a special relationship with the Buddha? The sunshine glimmering through the branches of the trees and the green pine needles contrasted sharply with these tired people.

Each deformed face tilted up to Monk Dasol as he continued. And I prayed for their souls to open up and embrace the compassion of the Buddha so that they may be born to better conditions in their next lives.

Monk Dasol did the best he could to try to make them understand, using analogies and metaphors where they could help. I watched his face and the faces of those listening to him. It seemed to me the most beautiful scene possible.

When Monk Dasol finished speaking, they bowed their heads reverently. "Master, would you recite the scriptures for us?"

Monk Dasol assumed the lotus position.

> I have betrayed the true nature
> And leaped into ignorance;
>
> I have been tainted by the colors and sounds
> Of birth and death;
>
> I have accumulated defilements
> By my ill temper and desires;
>
> I have sinned through seeing, hearing, tasting,

And drifted in the ocean of samsara;

I have been attached to myself and others,
And wandered astray in the evil ways;

To the power of the Three Treasures,
I sincerely repent,
The large and small sins
I have committed in my previous lives.

Monk Dasol's sorrowful voice resonated while women wiped away tears. After completing the recitation, he asked the people to pray with him to the Bodhisattva the Compassionate. He took out a small wooden bell he'd brought and began beating on the bell as he recited the name of the Bodhisattva the Compassionate, the people repeating after him. The wooden bell sounded through the forest, and the voices came sometimes as a chant, sometimes as a wail.

Would the Bodhisattva the Compassionate be looking upon them now? Oh, would the Bodhisattva the Compassionate be looking upon them now?

I felt a pang in my throat. The service among the pines came to a close. Monk Dasol stood.

"Master, how can we repay you for your grace?" said the woman.

"Thank you, Master. We can feel somewhat human again," the young man said.

The others remained silent, but their countenance said everything.

Monk Dasol smiled and said with feeling, "I thank all of you."

"You must be hungry," the young man said. His voice was halting, however.

"First, let me drink some water. If you have anything to eat, please bring it to me."

The young man's face brightened at seeing that Monk Dasol would eat with them. The others stirred in consultation, asking each other what they had to serve.

"Bring some potatoes," the young man asked one of the women, probably his wife. The woman stood up quickly, and the other women followed her.

With the women gone, there were only three people. Monk Dasol spoke easily with them on various topics. After some initial hesitation, the men talked about their hometowns, the leprosarium, the hog farms, and other things. From time to time, one would ask about current events in the outside world. Monk Dasol answered each question as best he could.

After some while, the young man's wife returned with a basket, which the man took and presented before us. Inside the basket was an aluminum bowl full of evenly shaped potatoes.

"Please have some." The young man placed the bowl in front of us.

"Yes, thank you. You, too, Bosal-nim," Monk Dasol said as he selected a potato.

"Thank you." I also began to eat.

There were some sidelong glances once in a while, so we were a little self-conscious about the meal, but we ate with full appetite. The conversation came easily during the meal, and by the time we were done eating, whatever hostility there was left toward me had gone also.

"Bosal-nim, shall we make a visit to the old woman?"

"Yes." I stood up to follow. The others did likewise.

"Where does she live?"

"Follow me." The young man led us to the old woman's hut. Inside, we found a gaunt old woman, lying on the floor like a larva in its cocoon.

"Are you sleeping? You have guests," the young man prompted. The woman, slowly and with effort, sat up. Her face had no nose, and her general appearance seemed to me what a monster in purgatory would look like. It was a miserable scene.

"Who is it?" She peered up in an attempt to look at us. Deep wrinkles creased her face, and her hands, fingerless, looked like dried roots. Her body was covered by clothes that had long ago lost their color. It looked like she lived in these clothes day and night, all four seasons of the year.

I looked at Monk Dasol, who stood silently. I took the clothes I'd bought and showed it to her. "Would you like to change into these clothes?"

The woman nodded but, otherwise, did not move.

"I'll help you." I held my hands out to her and began peeling off her old clothing. The stench of rotting flesh surrounded me, but I finished helping her out of her gown. It was difficult to believe this body was human, as abandoned as it was by human and divine hands.

"Would you wet this for me?" I handed a towel to the young man, who went out with it and quickly returned. The old woman's kitchen had long disintegrated with disuse. I opened the wet towel and sponged the woman's face and chest and arms. As I dressed her in her new skirt, I regretted that I had not brought underclothing. The old woman obeyed my instructions with childlike trust.

"Would you wait outside for a few minutes?"

The old woman looked at me once before hobbling out of the hut. I took out the disinfectant and cleaned into the small corners of the room as best I could.

Monk Dasol watched silently as I went about the hut, as did the young man. When I was ready to leave the hut, the young man hurried to arrange my shoes before me.

I thanked him and went out of the hut to where the old woman was crouched on the stoop.

"Goodbye."

At this, the old woman raised her hand in way of saying goodbye.

Monk Dasol and I went with the young man.

"Monk Dasol, I've brought some money. I thought I might leave it with the young man."

Monk Dasol looked at me but said nothing.

"They said they help the old woman with their earnings," I continued. "I think I can help, too."

"That would be a good idea," Monk Dasol said finally.

I quickly calculated how much it would cost for one month of food and handed it over to Monk Dasol, who, in turn, handed it to the young man.

"Bosal-nim is giving this for you to help the old woman. Please keep it and use it when you think she needs something," he said.

"The old woman lives by herself. She doesn't need much and has survived fine until now. Don't worry about her." The young man refused firmly.

"Monks believe it to be a sin to refuse a donation given by a sincere believer. Please accept this. I know you have hard times."

The young man accepted the money in resignation. I appreciated the fact that supporting the old woman was a burden they wanted to bear themselves.

The others gathered to see us off. "Where on earth can you find such wonderful people!"

"Goodbye."

"Will you come again?" the young man asked.

"I will." Monk Dasol clasped his hands, and they clasped their hands and bowed.

While walking back to the train station, I was left with the impression that I was returning from a faraway world. What world was it? In what universe?

"Mrs. Kang, would you like to go down to the stream to wash your hands?"

"It's Bosal-nim, isn't it?"

"Yes, Bosal-nim."

We laughed as we descended the bank to the water and dipped our hands in it. It was cool to the touch. I noticed that Monk Dasol was staring at my hands.

"It's hot. Why don't you wash your face, too?" I suggested.

I scooped the water with both hands and brought it to my face.

"Will you come again?" he asked.

"If you wish."

"I do."

I smiled, remembering.

Monk Dasol now sat on a big rock, looking up at the sky. He took out the wooden bell and began praying to the Bodhisattva the Compassionate. "Gwanseeum Bosal, Gwanseeum Bosal. . ." His voice and the clear sound of the wooden bell melted with the flowing of the stream.

Above his head, white clouds floated.

CHAPTER EIGHT:
August

I opened the window and lit a stick of incense. The incense burned slowly down, a lone thread of white smoke rising from it, a subtle fragrance spreading in the air where it rode the breeze. I lay in my bed and let myself go while I watched the smoke disappear into the air. It was a vacant and soothing experience.

It would be nice to die like this, I thought, and I wondered why I would think about death at a time like this.

The incense now burned to half its length, and my mind turned to my visit to Cheongsol. I should have burned incense in the old woman's room instead of spraying it with disinfectant. The old woman's face appeared in my mind's eye. Missing a nose and eyebrows and deeply wrinkled, it again brought images of monsters and purgatory. I remembered the foulness and the smell. Would I have been able to endure it were it not for Monk Dasol's watching eyes?

In teahouses and on buses, I occasionally encounter shabbily dressed people hawking chewing gum. Of course, they aren't in the business of selling gum but make their living through the sympathy of others. I always find it unpleasant to be around these people, but I'll usually pass over the money. I won't, however, accept the gum, and if someone were to ask me why, I would have to answer that this was not out of any generosity on my part, but because of my reluctance to put something handled by those people into my mouth.

I am that kind of woman. So, why was it so different under the watchful eyes of Monk Dasol? What power did he have over me? What had given me the courage to act like that? I closed my eyes and explored these questions carefully. For a moment, a realization came to me, but quickly my fear intervened and kept me from arriving at the answers.

"What are you up to, Mom?" Jaun smiled brightly.

"Not anything special."

"Enjoying your summer vacation?"

"Yes, very much."

Jaun was studying my face.

"Come," I said, patting the bed beside me.

She smiled and crawled into bed with me. I reached out an arm and placed it under her head.

"It's hot today," I said. "How would you like to go swimming?"

"I'd rather just stay like this."

"All day?"

"I don't think I could be any happier." Jaun touched my face with her fingertips, and her small hands warmed me.

The telephone rang, and Jaun got out of the bed, muttering who could be phoning at this time. After a few seconds, she was calling. "Mom, it's Aunt!"

I got up and took the receiver.

"Kihae, we're going to our cottage in Chosori tomorrow. I was hoping you could join us."

"Tomorrow?"

"Yes."

"For how long?"

"We have until Donghoon has to go back to school."

"I don't think so."

"Why not?"

"I have day duty at the school."

"Oh heavens, stop being so silly. You do too much for the measly amount you earn."

"That measly amount feeds three people."

"Cut it out. Jaun's father left a fortune."

"Don't," I warned.

"I'm sorry, Kihae. I shouldn't have said that."

"Have a nice time at the cottage."

"Kihae, how about Jaun?"

"By herself?"

"Why not?"

"Well…"

"Please, Kihae. It would be good for her and Donghoon to spend some time together. You know how lonely they are."

"I'll ask Jaun."

"Let me know."

I hung up the phone and went back to the bed, where Jaun was waiting for me.

"Is Aunt going somewhere?"

"To their cottage in Chosori."

"They're so lucky. It's by the ocean and there's that nice river, too."

"Would you like to go with them?"

"How about you, Mom?"

"I can't because of work."

"I wish you could stay at home like the other moms," she said sympathetically.

"I enjoy my time with the students."

Jaun looked but said nothing.

"I think it would be a good idea for you to go. You can play with Donghoon and the country air might do you some good."

"Do you think so?"

"You're going to have to get used to not having me around."

"What does that mean?"

"You're not going to live with me forever, are you?"

"What do you mean?" Jaun asked, wide-eyed. I felt an ominous cloud pass over us. I quickly changed the subject.

"I'll phone Aunt and tell her you're going. Go get ready."

Jaun left the room with a gloomy face while I went to phone my sister and pack a suitcase for Jaun.

After lunch, I was chatting with Jaun when I heard a car pull up to the house.

"Aunt's car is here," Dougienei called out.

Chapter Eight: August

I went out to the porch to greet my sister's driver. "Come in. I'm sorry to trouble you with Jaun on such a hot day."

"No, not at all. Is she ready?"

"Yes."

"Then I'll take her now."

"Won't you come in and have something cool to drink before you go?"

"No, thank you, I just had something and there's no room left." He chuckled.

There was nothing left to do then but to bring out the suitcase and send Jaun on her way. "Well, then, Jaun. Have a nice time, and I'll see you when you get home."

"I will, Mom." She looked close to tears but got in the car. I stood in the street, watching after them, long after they were gone.

"Why are you standing there like that? It's hot," Dougienei called. She'd come out to close the door.

The house was unbearably empty without Jaun there. But how much more must little Jaun feel when I'm not at home. I shook away the thought.

I went upstairs and, with nothing better to do, put a record on. The symphonic music of *The Sea*, by Claude Debussy, was soon coursing through the room. It brought images of the dawning sun, the brightening horizon, and finally the sunshine glimmering off the waves.

I woke to the ringing of the telephone. It was Jaun.

"Mom, we're just about to leave now."

"You sound happy, Jaun."

"I am. Take good care of yourself while I'm gone," she said, trying to cheer me up.

"I'll be fine. You have a nice time with Donghoon."

"I will. I'm hanging up now."

I put the receiver back in its cradle and went back to bed. I tried not to think of anything. I pulled up the covers and closed my eyes.

"There's a student here to see you."

I opened my eyes at Dougienei's voice. The clock read a few minutes past ten o'clock. "A student?"

"Yes, Hyegang is waiting downstairs."

"Hyegang?"

"Yes. I told him you were sleeping, so he said he would wait until you were up."

"You should have woken me sooner. Show him up, will you?" I dressed quickly and was washing my face when I heard Hyegang coming up the stairs. "Is that you, Hyegang?"

"Yes."

"Just a minute. I'll be right there." I came out drying my face with a towel.

Hyegang was dressed in old pants and a blue T-shirt.

"How have you been, Hyegang?"

"Fine, thank you. And you, Mrs. Kang?"

"I'm fine. Jaun left for the Chosori this morning. It's too bad you didn't come sooner."

"Chosori?"

"Yes, her aunt owns a cottage there."

"I see."

"Jaun would have liked to have seen you."

Hyegang looked out the window. As I watched him, it crossed my mind that he lived with Monk Dasol, eating, sleeping, talking with him, all under the same roof. The thought brought a tender feeling.

"Mrs. Kang?"

"Yes?"

"I was wondering if you would like to go to the Hongryun-am."

"What's that?"

"It's the cave where the Bodhisattva the Compassionate is said to be."

"Bodhisattva the Compassionate?"

"Yes."

"Where is it?"

"Near Naksan-sa Temple."

"Are you going by yourself?"

"I'm going with Monk Dasol?"

"With Monk Dasol?"

"Yes. He goes to the Hongryun-am each summer to pray."

"Each summer?"

"Yes. Until now, he has always gone alone, but this year, he invited me."

"This is a good opportunity for you. Go with him and pray hard."

"I would like for you to come with us, Mrs. Kang."

"You're going there to pray. How could I possibly go with you?"

"You can pray with us."

"Yes, but I'd better not."

"When I asked Monk Dasol whether I could invite you to come with us, he was silent at first, but then he told me to ask." He looked at me, uneasy at the thought that I might refuse him. His uneasiness urged me to go. I was also curious to see the cave.

"When do you leave?" I asked.

"Tomorrow, early in the morning."

"How long are you staying?"

"Three nights and four days."

"I'd probably just cause you a lot of trouble."

"So, you're coming?" His face turned hopeful.

"I'm thinking about it. Is Monk Dasol at the temple right now?"

"Yes. He doesn't go out or talk right before he leaves on a prayer retreat."

"I wish I could phone."

"Phone Monk Dasol?"

"Yes." I wanted to know if my coming would really be all right with him.

"I'll dial for you." Hyegang swept over to the phone and, after a moment, handed me the receiver with Monk Dasol on the line.

"Hello?"

"How have you been, Mrs. Kang?"

"Hyegang has asked me to join you on your trip to Hongryun-am, and I'm wondering if it would be all right with you."

"Perfectly. It might be good for you to find a special relationship with the Bodhisattva the Compassionate."

"I'll go then."

I hung up the phone and returned to my seat, slight excitement in my step.

"Mrs. Kang, we're leaving on the first bus tomorrow. We can meet at the terminal at six o'clock."

"All right."

Hyegang left, looking satisfied, and I found myself wondering what to pack. A prayer retreat was foreign to me. I had no idea what the occasion required.

I took out boxes of candles and incense, brushed the dust off them, and wrapped them in white rice paper. For offering, I took some money and put it in a white envelope. My preparations also included avoiding the radio and books. I wanted to keep my mind as clear as I could.

I woke early in the morning the next day, and washed myself in cold water. There was a certain sense to piety to everything I did, as I prepared to go on this retreat.

It was exactly six o'clock when I arrived at the bus terminal. As I made my way to the ticket office, Hyegang ran up to me. "I bought the tickets yesterday."

"Yesterday?"

"Yes. Monk Dasol sent me to buy for the three of us yesterday."

As Hyegang led me away, I saw the ash-colored robe of Monk Dasol as he sat quietly looking out the window.

"Good morning, Monk Dasol."

"Good morning, Mrs. Kang. Is this your first prayer retreat?"

"Yes, it is."

"It will be good for you."

It was time to board the bus.

"Hyegang, you sit there with your teacher." Monk Dasol pointed to a seat, while he took the seat in front of us. The bus slowly went on its way.

"Have you finished your statue of the Bodhisattva the Compassionate yet?"

"Not yet."

"Why not?"

"I can't visualize the image."

"I guess you'll be able to after this retreat."

Hyegang was silent.

Out the window, the landscape moved past and ahead loomed mountains. I glanced from the scenery at Monk Dasol's figure. He was motionless.

The rest of the trip went silently.

"You've had some difficulties, Mrs. Kang," Monk Dasol said as we stepped off the bus.

"Not at all."

"It has been said that it is better to know hardship when you attend a prayer retreat."

I smiled at his words.

We hailed a taxi, which went along the coast. The ocean stretched out from us on one side, dancing and alive. Watching it, I thought to myself, "That ocean is youth, such youth."

The taxi made a turn into a town and maneuvered through the tourists before climbing a hill. We got off at the peak, where the ocean rippled below.

"Over there is Hongryun-am," Monk Dasol said, pointing. "That is where Master Uisang met the Bodhisattva the Compassionate."

"Master Uisang lived more than thirteen hundred years ago. What brought him to such a remote place?" I asked.

"The Bodhisattva the Compassionate," he replied.

"Is this the only place where you can meet her?"

"In body, the Bodhisattva is not anywhere and cannot be seen. Her transformed essence, however, appears as an expedient means to the salvation of sentient beings. It is generally acknowledged that her essence resides in four places on earth: Mount Potalaka in India, the Small Training Center of Light Mountain in the South Seas, the Puji-si Temple of the island of Mount Putuo in China, and here."

"I see now that this is a sacred place. I wonder how Master Uisang came to meet the Bodhisattva."

"He was standing at the edge of the cliff, determined to throw himself into the sea if the Bodhisattva did not appear before him. There he prayed for seven days and seven nights. When those seven days and seven nights had passed and nothing had happened, he threw himself off the cliff. But a strange thing happened then. His body did not hit the water but was instead immersed in the Bodhisattva the Compassionate. He was happy, and he asked that she appear before him, so he could grasp her image. At that moment, a red lotus flower bloomed in the nearby cave, and there in the flower, sitting in the lotus position, was the brilliantly radiant essence of Bodhisattva the Compassionate."

"That's beautiful."

"Yes, beautiful," Monk Dasol repeated softly.

"Is the Bodhisattva still to be found here?"

"I believe so. I'm certain that if you pray faithfully, she will appear to you."

"How could I dare?" I looked at Monk Dasol and smiled.

We came down from the hill, listening to the sounds of the waves. The path to Hongryun-am before us filled me with a joy I could not explain. It was the feeling I had a few days ago as I watched the incense burn in my room.

At the foot of the hill, we came to the steps that led up to Hongryun-am. Bamboo groves lined along both sides, and through them, we could hear the waves. A strong quivering coursed through my body when we reached the courtyard. To be immersed in the Bodhisattva—it was a moving story.

Hyegang came to my side. "Mrs. Kang, shall we go in for a few minutes?"

I turned to find that Monk Dasol was talking with another man. I followed them inside, where through an opened door, we could see out into the ocean and hear the crashing of waves.

"Mrs. Kang, I'd like to introduce the resident priest of this temple," Monk Dasol said.

"How do you do?" I bowed from where I was sitting.

"It must have been a long and tiring trip," the priest said politely.

"Hyegang, please greet the priest, too," Monk Dasol said.

Hyegang bowed deeply twice. "Please accept my sincere regards."

"How long will you pray, Monk Dasol?"

"Three days."

"Will you be attending dawn services?"

"We will."

"Bosal-nim," the priest said, placing a white card in front of me. "Would you please fill out this prayer card?" When he saw me hesitate, he asked, "What is the name of your priest?"

"I'm sorry, I have no priest."

The resident priest looked slightly surprised. "What is your name then?"

"My name is Kihae Kang."

"You don't have a Buddhist name?"

"I don't."

"You haven't been initiated."

The cards were filled out in this way, one for me, one for Jaun. It was slightly embarrassing to be revealing my private life in this way with Monk Dasol watching, but we were soon finished and I thought it would be appropriate to take this time to present my offering.

"You must be hungry," said the resident priest as he left to have lunch prepared for us.

I watched the sun glinting off the ocean.

"Bosal-nim, your room has been prepared," the resident priest said when he returned. "It's the first one next to this building. You may want to rest before lunch."

"Thank you." I picked up my purse and stood up. Outside the sliding doors were three rooms built in a row, and I entered the one closest, and inside were five or six folded quilts placed in a stack and a pillow on top. I sat on the floor next to the wall and stretched out my legs. Even here, I could hear the waves. I wondered if it would be that loud at night.

"Bosal-nim, it's time for lunch." A lady attendant was standing in front of the door with a lunch tray.

After lunch, I came out to the courtyard. At the edge of the cliff overlooking the ocean grew wild roses. I descended a little way down the steps built into cliff, and looking down at the base where it met the water, I spotted a cave. "Maybe that's the one," I thought to myself. I looked at the water and breathed deeply. It was a long way down.

"That might be the Bodhisattva Bird."

I hadn't noticed Hyegang behind me. He was pointing at a bird.

"The Bodhisattva Bird?" I asked.

"Yes. The bird that guided Master Uisang to this spot."

"How did it do that?"

"During Master Uisang's search, there appeared a blue bird. This bird, flying from tree to tree, guided the master, who knew that he was to follow it."

I looked at the bird Hyegang was pointing to. It was small like a swallow, blue in the back and purple-chested. I studied the little bird. From its perch on the edge of the cliff, the bird cocked its head to one side and met my gaze.

"Are you harking my arrival here, too?" I thought, and smiled to myself.

The waves rushed at the cliff, surging at the cave before crashing into the rock. I watched the waves continue their barrage over and over again.

"Hyegang, will you let me see your statue when you're finished?"

"I don't think I'll ever finish it."

"Pray your best. This is the place for it, isn't it?"

Hyegang grinned back at me.

It was the afternoon and time for the monks to gather in the main hall for worship services. Monk Dasol's ceremonial robe spoke dignity. As the monks entered the hall, Hyegang lit the candles and incense and changed the water in preparation for the ceremony. The monks bowed and prayed to the Bodhisattva.

> The greatly compassionate Bodhisattva Avalokiteśvara!
>
> We believe with all our hearts in the efficacy of your appearance as an expedient means to teach us and in the power of your vows to save us. Oh, Gwanseeum Bosal.

Feeling rose in my heart with the chanting, which now moved from the *Heart Sutra* to the *Thousand Hands Sutra*. I closed my eyes, taking in the sutra recitations that now mingled with the sounds of the ocean in the air. The

Buddhas and the bodhisattvas of the universe—did they hear our earnest pleas?

After the recitations, the monks stood and began chanting the name of the Bodhisattva: "Gwanseeum Bosal, Gwanseeum Bosal…"

I repeated after them, my eyes on the figure that stood in the hall against the ocean background. At various times, it smiled; sometimes, it looked down with fury; at other times, it glared.

What was the source of these metamorphoses? The way the light was hitting it? Or was the shifting expression nowhere but in my own mind?

Monk Dasol's wooden bell sounded through the hall. Hyegang stood in the corner of the hall, looking up at the Bodhisattva the Compassionate. His face was pale in the afternoon light.

What could Monk Dasol be praying for? Hyegang? We kneeled before the Bodhisattva sadly and humbly. The Bodhisattva's compassion and sympathy, was this divine pity for the pitiful?

"Gwanseeum Bosal, Gwanseeum Bosal…"

The chanting lasted for two hours, until Monk Dasol put away his wooden bell and bowed one last time to the Bodhisattva. I felt the subtle beauty in Monk Dasol, as he bowed deeply, his hands held together in front of him.

With services now over, Monk Dasol turned to us, his hands still clasped. "Attain the Buddhahood."

I brought my own hands together and echoed his words. "Attain the Buddhahood."

"Attain the Buddhahood."

With that, Monk Dasol left the hall. Hyegang maintained his contemplation of the Bodhisattva, and then finally extinguishing the candles, he motioned for me to leave. I nodded.

Seagulls littered the late afternoon ocean, its waves shining silver-gray. I inhaled deeply and stood with the scene in front of me.

How do you define an ocean's nature? It nurtures lives even as it destroys others. Where is it in water that gives it the power to nurture? What part of it is it that destroys?

The seagulls flocked over the ocean, some soaring into the sky, some diving toward the water. Do these seagulls exist only to eat? Do they accumulate nothing but the bad karma of killing living things? Have they been given life themselves only to sin?

I spent the afternoon before main services cleaning the main hall. I dusted the altar with a dry cloth, swept, and mopped the wood floor. I emptied the ceremonial vessel into a bucket, took the bucket to the window, and poured the water into the ocean, where I hoped the fish and whales would benefit from it. I took the bucket out to the well and refilled it for the ceremonial vessel. I lit the candles and incense I'd brought from home.

Afterwards, I went back to the window and looked out to the ocean. Darkness fell slowly.

Soon the ocean will be shrouded in the darkness and I will no longer be able to see its shape. Isn't this like life? When the darkness arrives, physical life disappears. But just as the ocean has a basic nature that doesn't change in the night, is there a fundamental nature in the lives of people that remains constant through life and death? A life that will never belong forever to the darkness, one that does not depend on illusion—is the life of the Buddha?

That life and death is not separate, that there is a ground of life, a suchness in itself, that transcends expansion or contraction—the concepts were still vague, but I knew they'd become meaningful in my life.

The monks, dressed in their ceremonial robes, entered the main hall for evening services. Monk Dasol looked ahead, stern as ice, his eyes sharp and bright. The monks stood before the Bodhisattva and struck their wooden bells, slowly reciting the passages of adoration, before bowing once more. I followed suit.

Night fell outside, and the candlelight grew brighter. Reverent awe filled me as I watched the silhouettes of the monks.

Do these monks go down the lonely path in hopes of ridding themselves of ignorance, that which causes suffering?

As I watched Monk Dasol, I thought about a story I'd read a long time ago about the Gautama Buddha's experience of awakening.

> At that moment... as dawn was breaking
> and the ghosts were going to their resting
> places, the great seer attained the infinite,
> and the leader achieved knowledge of
> all. In reverence of the Buddhahood, the
> earth swayed like a woman drunk on
> wine, the sky shone bright with Siddhas,

and the mighty breezes blew softly, rain
fell from a cloudless sky, flowers and
fruits dropped from empty trees... The
great seers could be heard proclaiming
his fame.

Would such a splendid moment come to this monk? Is
he now burning his body for that moment? Is the body in
the way of that awakening experience?

At midnight, Monk Dasol set his wooden bell aside
and, with hands clasped, bowed to the Bodhisattva. He
turned to us and, as before, said, "Attain the Buddhahood."
He left the main hall, and Hyegang and I followed.

A cold waning moon hung in the black sky, its light
shining off the ocean waves, which were even louder in
the night. As I lay in my room, I heard the roar in the
dark, the crashing of waves. It gave the sensation that I
was floating on the water.

The prayer retreat lasted for three days, and over that
short period, I accepted the Bodhisattva into my heart.
She became a source of support for me—not only support,
but also a source of joy and faith. I saw the Bodhisattva
the Compassionate as someone I could believe in.

On the afternoon of the second day, I was walking
in the courtyard when passing in front of Monk Dasol's
room, I could see him through the bamboo screen that
hung in the doorway. He was sitting over Hyegang, who
was sleeping, and from a bottle, he was applying a salve
on the boy's arms, probably to treat mosquito bites. He
rubbed the salve and was blowing on it as he did. I was
touched by the scene: a father tenderly looking over his

sleeping child. At our first meeting, I'd once remarked that if Hyegang were indeed a child fallen from the heavens, Monk Dasol would be his father. I remember his reply: "You may be right." It was obvious to me that Hyegang was growing strong under Monk Dasol's love for him. I felt human affection.

The monk's heart is warm. He is well versed in the ways of human love.

Careful not to be seen, I returned to my room. I lay down, listening to the sounds of the crashing waves below. Breathing deeply, I felt my body, weary and withered like an ancient tree, growing alive again. The physical change in me brought also a little fear. "What is to become of me? Where am I going?"

I was resting in my room after dinner when Monk Dasol came to my door. "There is a special worship service at dawn tomorrow. If you're not too tired, I would like to invite you to attend the intrepid prayer tonight in preparation."

I'd never heard of an intrepid prayer, but imagining it to be some sort of all-night vigil, I said I would be there.

The evening service began as the ocean faded into the darkness. Candles illuminated the main hall. Monk Dasol, as he did the day before, recited the name of the Bodhisattva to the beat of his wooden bell. At midnight, Hyegang and others left the hall, leaving only Monk Dasol and me. I had the sudden urge to hold his hand.

Wiping the thought from my mind, I prayed sincerely and earnestly for the Bodhisattva to give me strength. The ocean moved in the darkness outside. I closed my eyes to the sound of restless waves.

Tok, tok. Monk Dasol's wooden bell rang in the darkness. When I opened my eyes again, Monk Dasol was still standing, his hand striking the wooden bell, but otherwise motionless. The clock on the altar read half past two. Monk Dasol turned to me. "You have not been initiated."

"No."

"Would you like to be initiated now?"

"What does it mean to be initiated?"

"It is to become a disciple of Buddha. The rite is complicated but only of secondary importance. What is important is your willingness."

"I would like to be initiated."

Monk Dasol looked at me in silence before speaking again. "This is where the red lotus flower appeared so many years ago. It would be appropriate, then, for you to adopt 'Haeryun' as your Buddhist name. It means 'Lotus Flower of the Sea.'"

I said nothing.

"It is difficult to live up to Buddhist ideals. But I hope you try your best." Monk Dasol picked up an incense stick and lit it with one of the candles. He brought it to me and held the glowing red end to my arm, his other hand lightly touching the tips of my fingers.

"When you feel the sting, all your accumulated sins will disappear," he said with a soft smile. Then he took the rosary from around his neck and placed it around mine. "I hope you will cherish this for a long time. Whenever you find yourself in difficult times, you may call to the Bodhisattva the Compassionate."

I felt a hot teardrop run down my cheek. I bit my lip and bowed my head, Monk Dasol looking down on me.

I wanted to throw myself into his chest and cry completely. I wanted this as much as I'd ever wanted anything. Monk Dasol looked at me in silence for a moment, then said "Gwanseeum Bosal," and sighed.

Monk Dasol picked up the wooden bell and began the recitation of the Bodhisattva the Compassionate. I joined in, our two voices sounding like a litany of sobbing.

Guilt overran me, as I thought about how much pain I was causing him. In an attempt to escape it, I walked over to the candles and incense and returned with ones newly lit.

At this, Monk Dasol closed his eyes and began to strike his wooden bell with more urgency, tiny beads of perspiration on his face.

Dawn began to push the darkness away from the sea. Monk Dasol stood up, picked up a mallet, and rang the metal bell. Its sound flew away over the ocean waves.

CHAPTER NINE:

September

Sunlight hung over the schoolyard like a bleached white cloth, and with it, there was the tinge of autumn air.

Autumn used to be my favorite season. Everything was so clear this time of year, and its smell was a like a breath of fresh air for the soul. The season was usually a time of planning for me, a time to look forward. But these days, its arrival brought a subtle pang of sadness and slight dread, a feeling that had been building for some time.

"Mrs. Kang, you look like you've lost some weight," the fine arts teacher said warily.

"Well, I'm getting older."

"Older? You look like a young girl."

"You were saying before how I had a child's emotions. Now you're saying I even look like a girl."

"Yes, just like a young girl, the way you see and the way you look."

"What a strange thing to say. Do I seem that childish?"

"Not childish, really. More like childlikeness or something. I mean, you're not stale, like adults are."

"I don't think I understand. It sounds like a compliment and an insult at the same time."

I thought about what the fine arts teacher said after he left the room. It was absurd to think that a woman in her thirties could still be a child. But he was right to think I was not grown up. I had never developed the ambitions that usually come with maturity. For me, there was no real design to my life, no faraway goals or things I wanted. I had only a vague idea that life should be spent in preparation for death. I hoped to die knowing that I had lived well.

If I did aspire to anything, it was to see things with deeper insight—to see things and know their significance—which I agree sounds like a highly abstract goal to be striving for. Trying to achieve it was like trying to touch a fluffy cloud in the sky. Again and again, I reached for it, only to find that its closeness was only an illusion, and I would turn away in dejection, like a defeated soldier. Over and over again—my endeavors were the one constant in my life, the one symbol of continuity. But the defeats wore away at me, and each new experiment was made with lesser expectations. My heart no longer pounded with anticipation.

It was around this time I met Monk Dasol, an honest man. Even then, I could see that his soul was untainted. I'd heard it as a breeze blowing deep in the mountains. It was what I'd been yearning for. But Monk Dasol had kept his distance, and so did I, if not geographically, emotionally. It was not in my power to narrow the gap between us.

"What are you thinking, Mrs. Kang."

"Excuse me?" I snapped out of my musings. It was Mrs. Hahn.

"You look like you're thinking about something. What are you thinking about?" Mrs. Hahn looked at me with a scrutinizing expression. I felt the intrusion and was slightly offended by it.

"I heard we're getting one hundred percent bonuses this month, on account of the Chuseok holidays," she said.

"Is that right? That'll be something to appreciate."

"The Bear is trying to save face, see?"

The Bear was what we called the chairman of the board of directors. I ignored the remark, tired of puns.

There were teachers already lined up by the time we got to the payroll office. Mrs. Hahn and I stood behind them. I remembered my first paycheck. I'd thought it was disgraceful for a person to have to wait in line for money and had returned the next day, after everybody had received their checks. That was a long, long time ago.

The teachers were bright and cheery after a long month of low funds. Despite their lofty ideals regarding education, they were very much yoked to the system.

I returned to the staff room, paycheck in hand. We'd been paid the equivalent of four months' salary as a bonus, the first time anything like this had happened. It was a windfall. I was wondering how I was going to spend it when Mrs. Hahn approached me. "Mrs. Kang, I'm going shopping. Want to come?"

"What are you buying?"

"I want to buy a carpet. The one we have is a few years old and its color is fading. I thought I'd buy a new one."

"Mine is still in pretty good condition."

"But maybe you'd like to replace it, just for a change."

Mrs. Hahn's comment struck me as odd. The concept of spending money "just for a change" was an unfamiliar one to me. Then it occurred to me that I had lived a long time as a single woman. The recognition saddened me, but it was true. The reason for my unenthusiastic approach to life wasn't just because of my character, but also because of my present circumstances.

"My carpet will do fine," I said. Not only did I not want a new carpet, but the thought of spending an extended period of time with her was repellent. Mrs. Hahn accepted my refusal and left.

The staff room was buzzing today. Some of the teachers had removed their paychecks from the envelopes and were calculating the amounts, while others had just deposited them into their pockets, a look of well-being on their face. Obvious here was the power of money as a lubricant of life.

"Mrs. Kang, aren't you going home?" the fine arts teacher asked.

"I am."

"Let's go." He stood up. I picked up my purse and walked with him out of the school.

"What a windfall we got today. I can't wait to spend it."

"Spend? Maybe you should go home first."

"Wait, let me think how I can spend it so that it'll do the most good." His face brightened with expectation. The words he used, "do the most good," reminded me suddenly of Cheongsol, and along with it, the old woman's withered face. Right then I decided my bonus should go to helping the people of Cheongsol. The thought filled my heart with excitement.

After parting with the fine arts teacher, I stopped in at the teahouse and, over a cup of tea, thought over the matter again. It still appeared to me to be the best way of using the money. Chuseok, the Korean Thanksgiving, was only a few days away. The money could go a long way toward making the holiday a happy one for these people. The idea made me feel like a powerful woman, and I smiled.

It would be presumptuous of me to make the decision without consulting Monk Dasol, I thought, given that my relationship with Cheongsol was through him. But it was too late to call him at his office, so I decided to call him at the temple when I got home.

Jaun fluttered to me like a butterfly as I got off the bus.

"Have you been waiting long?" I asked.

"It's not so bad since it got cool."

"It was bad when it was hot?"

Jaun only smiled.

We spent a peaceful supper together. I marveled at how quickly Jaun was maturing into a thoughtful and delicate young woman.

After supper, I dialed the phone number Hyegang had given me long ago. Monk Dasol's voice answered low and quiet.

"How are you, Monk Dasol? This is Hyegang's teacher."

"I recognized your voice. How are you?"

"I received some money I was expecting today, and while I was thinking about how I was going to spend it, I thought of Cheongsol. With Thanksgiving coming, I'd like to spend it on them. I wonder what you think of the idea."

"Wonderful. A similar idea crossed my mind today, as a matter of fact. Let's do something like that."

"You were thinking the same thing?"

"If you, Bosal-nim, a laywoman, were that considerate, so how much more should a monk be?" He chuckled.

"I was a little apprehensive about the money, but knowing that you were thinking the same thing makes me feel that it's all right."

"Why would you be apprehensive? Good things are always good, aren't they?"

"What should we do now?"

"Well, I'm in the middle of writing a paper, so I won't be free for some time."

"Then will you send the money with Hyegang? I'll go to Cheongsol by myself."

"That sounds fine with me. I'll send the money tomorrow."

We said goodbye and I hung up.

I went to bed thinking about my plans to go to the pig farm this Saturday. In the middle of this, a sudden wave of exhaustion passed over me and a familiar twist of pain gripped me inside. Soon it was gone.

I left for Cheongsol on Saturday with two envelopes: one from Monk Dasol, one from me. At the train station there, I asked where I could find the pig farm, and following the directions I was given, I came to a neat-looking building that looked slightly like a university dormitory. As they'd said, it looked a much better place to live than the huts in the village.

After looking around inside, a familiar face greeted me.

"Do you work here?"

"Yes, but what are you doing here?" she asked, surprise on her face. Her blue work clothes reminded me of a prison uniform.

"I'm looking for that young man who met us last time."

"You mean Supervisor Choi? What do you want to see him for?"

"I have something to give him."

"Just a minute, please." She hurried off and returned with Supervisor Choi, along with several other people, apparently curious why I was there.

"What a surprise," the young man greeted me, a broad smile on his face.

"I didn't have much time, so that's why I came directly here."

"What is it?"

"With the Chuseok holiday coming, Monk Dasol and I have prepared a gift for you. This is some money we came by quite unexpectedly. Please accept it."

The villagers looked on silently while I handed the envelopes to the young man.

"We make enough money by working. We'd rather that you remember us and visit from time to time."

"Of course, we'll come again. But also we wanted to do something for you for the holiday. Please accept the money."

There was some audible stirring in the group.

Supervisor Choi considered for a moment before speaking. "We accept with the greatest gratitude." I put the envelopes into his deformed hands, which despite their deformity at that moment looked quite beautiful to me. He opened the envelopes for the people to see and, seeing how much there was, expressed his surprise. "This is too much."

"It's a big holiday. I hope you will be able to prepare some special food with the money."

Supervisor Choi considered the envelopes for another moment, then: "Thank you very much. We will have the biggest feast we have ever had in our lives. To tell you the truth, each time this year comes, we cry inside. While everyone else visits their parents' graves to pay their respects, we can't, looking like we do."

The villagers' grief was visible. The reminder must have been painful for them to hear.

"Yes," I said. "Have a big feast and enjoy the holiday."

"I hope you and Monk Dasol can join us."

"We'll try."

"Don't just try. Please be sure to be with us," Supervisor Choi said.

Smiling at his insistence, I promised to come and turned to leave. I felt their gaze on my back for a long time as I walked away. Later, it occurred to me that the woman who had first asked Monk Dasol to pray for the dead woman that day was not among the group. Maybe she was the peddler that Supervisor Choi mentioned.

Chapter Nine: September

The mornings and the evenings were quite cool now, making the commute between the school and home much easier to bear. But the realization that autumn was here made me melancholy.

I stopped in at the open-air market on the way home from school for groceries and rice cakes, the latter to use as an offering for my late husband. As I left, I reminded myself to have the rice merchant deliver some of this year's harvest.

At the entrance to the market were street-side stalls selling clothes. With the weather becoming cooler these days, they reminded me that Jaun would need some fall clothes. I browsed through a few of the stalls and, finding a sweater I thought she'd like, made a mental note to return for it the next day.

Jaun was not there when I got off the bus. She had gone with her Girl Scout troops to visit a nursing home and must not have got back yet. I was walking up the hill toward my house alone, carrying the things I'd bought at the market, when I almost fainted. It was as if all the energy in my body had disappeared. And there was a pain in my chest, which, by the time it stopped, had left me soaked with perspiration.

Foreboding flashing through my mind, I was afraid, and I shook my mind free of bad thoughts. But the bag I was carrying had become too heavy. I didn't think I'd be able to carry it home.

With no other option, I left the bag with a nearby store and went home without it. There, I collapsed into my bed and sank into it and to the earth. It felt like the final sinking into death. Unwilling to accept this, I struggled up and splashed cold water on my face.

"How about the rice?" I heard Dougienei calling from downstairs.

"Will you ask the merchant to deliver a sack?" I thought about the sacrifice rituals to be held tomorrow. There would be two: one upstairs for my husband; after that, another one downstairs for Doug's father. It bordered on the inappropriate to have two rituals under the same roof, but I took it as my responsibility to help Doug, now a man, carry out his filial duties.

I went into the kitchen to fry the vegetables and wash the fruit. While I was preparing the offering, the image of my husband's face came back to me. We had spent six years together, but since his death, he'd become a dim memory. It was sometimes difficult to remember what he looked like. It had been eight years ago that he'd died. Jaun had been five.

Although there had been no particularly strong affection between us, I always believed, and believe now, that he was a good man. If he were still alive now, it would have been domestic bliss. It was difficult to imagine how time had stolen my memories of him.

Despite the guilt I felt over this, I did not visit my husband's grave at Chuseok. This was not just because he was buried in Chung-nam Province. I couldn't bear it that Jaun, who missed her father so much, would see only her father's grave, not her father.

Jaun came back late in the afternoon. "Mom, I sang 'Spring in My Home Village' at the nursing home."

"The grandmothers and grandfathers must have liked it."

"Like? Oh, Mom. I shouldn't have sung. Some of them cried when I sang."

"Because it reminded them of their hometowns."

"When I saw the tears on their faces, I started crying, too."

As I listened to Jaun talking about her day at the nursing home, I became aware that Jaun was no longer a small girl.

Doug joined us as we sat down for dinner. He'd become a new man, his face now beaming confidence.

"How do you like the job, Doug?" I asked.

"Great."

"No problems?"

"None at all."

Dougienei came out of the kitchen with a bowl of rice for Doug. Apparently, she had been expecting her son to come home for Chuseok.

Doug looked up at his mother. "You've been all right, Mother?"

"What did you expect, that I'd be dead?"

I laughed inside, wondering why Dougienei insisted on being so tasteless. We began eating. Doug and Jaun chatted, catching up on each other's news.

Sometime during dinner, the pain erupted again in my chest. I waited for it to pass, my teeth clenched firmly. Doug looked at me with concern on his face. Fortunately, Jaun didn't notice and went on with her dinner. When the pain disappeared, it went completely and I was able to continue.

"I was thinking it would be nice to give offering to Doug's father this year as well as to Jaun's father," I said.

"My father?"

"Yes. Until now, you were too young or you were in the army. But now that you're a grown man, I think it's time to do this for your father."

Doug stayed silent, but Dougienei's eyes broke into a smile. "It's considerate of you to think of it." Although she hadn't said it, it must have been almost unbearable for her to have to spend the holiday without doing this for her deceased husband.

"We'll have two services tomorrow. Auntie, will you prepare two sets of fruit? I think we have enough for both."

Dougienei, an awkward smile on her face, went into the kitchen. Jaun was tired from her trip today and went up to her room soon after dinner.

When it was just the two of us left in the room, Doug looked at me nervously. "Mrs. Kang, are you sick?"

"I don't know. Sometimes, my chest hurts."

"Since when?"

"Only recently."

Doug was clearly worried. "I'll be back here in a month. If the pain is still there, I'd like to take you to the hospital."

"We'll see when the time comes." I went upstairs to my room to make arrangements for the next day. In the morning, I would give offering and afterwards send Jaun over to my sister's. In the afternoon, I would go

Chapter Nine: September

to Cheongsol. I'd agreed to meet Monk Dasol at Seoul Station at three o'clock. We would arrive in Cheongsol at five. It would be late by the time we got back, but there was no other choice.

The next day, we arrived in Cheongsol slightly past five, as expected. We made our way along the now familiar path. The villagers were in a relaxed and jovial mood. As we passed the well to where the huts sat, they came out to meet us, each expressing their gratitude.

"I was worried you wouldn't come, but you're really here."

"Oh, Master, it's late." Supervisor Choi and the woman stepped up to us in welcome.

As we entered the courtyard, there were two men, placed on either side of a thick wooden block, pounding dough with big wooden mallets. I looked on with interest.

"We rarely give offering, even on Chuseok, so we didn't have rice cakes this morning. And we assumed you wouldn't arrive until late in the afternoon, so we didn't start making them until just a while ago," Supervisor Choi was saying.

The two men continued to pound in rhythm.

"Why don't you just buy some at the rice cake shop in town?"

"We could do that. But if we do, people think we're defiling their sacrificial food, and the owner doesn't like us either."

"On Chuseok, the dough is shaped into half-moons and steamed on a layer of pine needles," I mentioned.

"I know. But without fingers, we can't make those delicate shapes. There's a lot we can't do, as you can see. We can't go home to pay respects to our ancestors either. So we have to make our rice cakes this way, and we have to piece together our childhood memories by ourselves. We find our own ways to soothe away our loneliness."

Judging by his diction, I guessed that Supervisor Choi had completed at least a grade twelve education. He was a natural leader, with an ability to deal with things as they arose. His words and actions were composed and wise.

The women were busily at work around the village. Some were frying foods, some were roasting, some broiling, some arranging washed fruit in a basket. A festive atmosphere whistled and bustled between the huts.

Around six o'clock, the women brought the prepared food to the courtyard. Rice cakes and newly harvested rice in a large wooden bucket, taro soup steaming in a pot. Ladled into individual dishes were road bellflower roots, fern brakes, dried eggplant, radishes, green bean sprouts, mushrooms—all prepared in the most appetizing way. All looked delicious. Pears, apples, and steamed chestnuts were also brought out in a basket.

A large nylon mat, apparently prepared especially for this occasion, was spread out in the courtyard. On it, the villagers laid out the dishes of food and, after finishing with the preparations, went into their huts. They returned in new clothes. Curiously, most wore white. The general tendency was to wear bright and colorful clothes on such days, but these people wore white.

"It's a big feast." Monk Dasol smiled.

"We prepared meat, too. But we know monks don't eat meat, so we didn't bring it out. We'll eat that later." Supervisor reported this as if to account for how they spent the money. Then he announced, "Tonight, we'll have a *han* exorcism."

"What is a *han* exorcism?" I asked.

"We are people filled with resentment and grievances against the unfairness of life. This *han* remains in our hearts like a lump. Tonight, we release it."

"I see."

"Let's have this feast that Master and Bosal-nim prepared for us. Let's have our fill. And then we will resolve this *han* in our hearts," Supervisor Choi said to the villagers.

The feast began. People placed food before Monk Dasol and me for us to eat. They ate their meals with relish, talking and laughing over their food. After the meal was over and we'd pushed our tray away, I said to Monk Dasol, "I'm afraid it's time for us to leave."

"Yes, we should go."

Monk Dasol was about to stand when Supervisor Choi tugged on his sleeve and said, "Master, please, spend tonight—only tonight—with us here. Help us to resolve the *han* accumulated in our hearts." His voice was earnest and pleading. Monk Dasol and I looked at each other.

"Bosal-nim," the young man continued. "You stay with us, too, please. The law of causation has brought you to us. Please spend one night here."

The people looked on with eyes full of feeling.

Monk Dasol turned to me. "Tomorrow is Sunday. What do you think, Bosal-nim?"

I rarely spent the night outside of my home. But I was curious about *han* exorcisms and I was not bold enough to refuse their pleading. I accepted the invitation.

"Thank you. Now let's enjoy ourselves," Supervisor Choi said. Over the pine grove on the hill, the bright full moon of Chuseok began its ascent into the clear night sky.

A few of the villagers piled wood in the middle of the courtyard and began a bonfire. The pine now burning brightly, the peddler woman stood up and began to sing:

> Oh, it's you, it's you,
> It's really you.
>
> It's you, who fretted over the disease,
> That rotted your healthy body.
>
> Is it because of fate
> That we meet like this
> After so many months?
>
> Here I've come, here I've come,
> Oh, here I've come.
>
> Here I've come
> From a thousand miles away from home,
> Blown by the winds,
> Carried by the clouds,
> Here I've come.
>
> Why have I come here?
> It's to see you, oh, my dear...

She sang in a sorrowful voice while her body rocked and swayed. The others watched her and kept beat with their hands. The woman spun her body lightly and swiftly, as if possessed. The white sleeves of her clothes reached into the air in a wide arc, as if embracing the moon. Monk Dasol and I watched breathlessly.

When she finished, she sank to the ground and a man stood up. He motioned for the others to join him as he began into "Kwaejina Chingching."

The mood built in a crescendo, stronger and stronger. Another man stood up after the other had sat down, and sang "Gang'gang Suwollae." The others echoed the refrain as he sang:

> The sun has set, and the moon is rising
> —Gang'gang Suwollae.
>
> Set up a loom in the sky
> —Gang'gang Suwollae.
>
> Spin threads out of the clouds
> —Gang'gang Suwollae.
>
> Make a shuttle out of the moon
> —Gang'gang Suwollae.
>
> Sprinkle the stars into patterns
> —Gang'gang Suwollae.
>
> Click, click, weaving nicely
> —Gang'gang Suwollae.

What shall we do with the cloth
—Gang'gang Suwollae.

When my brother gets married
—Gang'gang Suwollae.

I'll wrap it around the chair in his sedan
—Gang'gang Suwollae.

The moon was at its zenith now, and the night dew was damp like tears. More pine wood was added onto the fire, and people began to dance by the firelight. If anyone sang out an expression of his *han,* the people repeated after.

The *han* exorcism was approaching its climax as people sang and danced out their *han.* As I watched them, my heart wept.

After midnight, the villagers slowly began taking their places around the fire, some to fall asleep there. Monk Dasol and I leaned against a pine tree at the rim of the courtyard and stared blankly at the fire.

What is life?

The peddler woman came to Monk Dasol. "Master, will you recite the scripture for us?" Her eyes were moist with tears.

"Will you bring me a gourd dipper?"

The woman swiftly went away to the well and came back with a pail filled with water. She placed the gourd dipper upside down into it. Monk Dasol closed his eyes and, holding the dipper with one hand, began striking it with the other:

In my next lives,
May I grow in Buddha's wisdom.

Whenever I may be born again,
May I meet with wise teachers
In a good world.

May I be firm in the right faith
So that I may renounce the worldly life
In my childhood.

May my hearing and sight be clear,
May my words be sincere.
May I be free from the defilement
of worldly things,

May I practice the discipline of the clean life
So that I may not violate even
the most minor rule.

I will love all forms of life with dignity,
And I will protect them even at
the sacrifice of my own life.

The light of the moon bathed the courtyard in white. The faces that now looked upon Monk Dasol were clear in their beauty.

Oh, Dawn,
May thou not come.

Oh, cruel Dawn,
Who bringest bodies into the bright light,
May thou not come.

I prayed in my heart.

Monk Dasol embraced the pail now full with moon-light and recited the Buddhist prayer of aspiration. His voice rode higher with the moonlight into the night sky.

CHAPTER TEN:

October

After closing session, Hyegang came to me in the staff room. "Mrs. Kang, I have something to tell you," he said.

"What is it?"

"I can't tell you here. Can we go someplace quieter?"

"Where? Should we go to the counselors' office?"

"That's too stuffy. How about the bench under the maidenhair tree?"

"That would be fine," I said. "You go ahead. I'll meet you there shortly."

Hyegang left the staff room. I closed the *Flower Garland Sutra* I'd been reading and went into the schoolyard.

The leaves on the maidenhair tree had turned golden and were fantastically beautiful in the autumn light.

I wish people, too, could die so beautifully. But human death is always ugly. The dead body left behind is ugly. I wish that we could disappear without a trace, even if we could not leave this world as beautifully as the leaves on the maidenhair tree.

"Mrs. Kang, do you think our lives are determined by fate?"

"Well, there are those who boldly claim they control their own fate."

"Even if we cannot choose the size of our clothes, we can choose the color."

"The size of our clothes is fated?"

"Yes," Hyegang replied. "So to speak."

"What made you think of that, Hyegang?"

"I wish to choose the best color for my fate."

"What color is that?"

"Gray, the color of a sacred robe."

"A sacred robe?"

"I've decided that my fate would look most beautiful dressed in the gray color of a sacred robe."

Not knowing what to say, I waited for Hyegang to continue. He was looking up at the blue sky.

"How did you decide this?" I asked finally. "Isn't it too early to make this sort of decision yet?"

"I think the decision was already made for me when I was little, maybe even when I was born."

"What will you do?"

"Tomorrow, I will be initiated as an apprentice monk."

"To be a monk might in fact be the way for you, but you don't need to rush into it, do you? If it is meant to be, you will become a monk anyway."

"Now that my path is clear, I don't think I need to go through experimenting."

"What do you mean by experimenting?

"To love somebody, to grow attached with somebody, like that."

"If you love, you should love, I think. Is there something wrong with loving somebody?"

"There's nothing wrong with it for others. But it's wrong for me."

"Why just for you?"

"Because I might be a leper."

"Why do you think that way? The medical tests have shown that's not the case."

"Even medical science cannot predict who will or who won't suffer."

"But that doesn't mean you should decide the course of your life based on speculation and guessing."

"Ten years from now, if I wanted to marry Jaun, would you let me?"

The question was completely unexpected. Why was he asking it? Was he taking Jaun just as an example, or was there something in his heart for her?

"I'm sorry, Mrs. Kang."

I remained silent.

"Will you attend the initiation ceremony tomorrow?"

"What does Monk Dasol have to say about this?"

"He said we should make the decision after some time has passed."

"So, why are you rushing into it?"

"I made the decision at Hongryun-am." Hyegang would not be shaken from his resolve. As he'd said, it might not be necessary for him to go through the processes of trying and experimenting if this path he'd chosen was in fact right for him.

"What time tomorrow?" I asked.

"Ten o'clock in the morning."

"I'll be there." There was great heaviness in my heart as I said goodbye to Hyegang.

Hyegang saw love as an experiment. And all pain is said to come from personal attachment, and attachment comes from being close with another.

I spent most of the night tossing and turning, confused by how the best way to avoid pain was to avoid growing close to somebody. But only those who have experienced life could know this. It seemed cruel to be imposing it on a young boy. Early in the morning, I left the house and caught the bus for Jeongreung. At the bus terminal, I took the mountain road and, after about a half hour, reached Yeongdeung-sa Temple. The ceremony had already begun when I stepped into the courtyard.

In front of Hyegang was a large basin of ceremonial water. Hyegang stood up and bowed twice each to the deities of the heaven and earth in the East, the West, the South, and the North. Then he bowed to Monk Dasol, the man who had raised him up to this point. Standing, eyes lightly closed, Monk Dasol accepted the bow.

Following this, Monk Dasol dipped his hands in the water and sprinkled it over Hyegang's head. He picked up a pair of scissors and made three cuts in Hyegang's locks. Then the Master of Truth and the Master of Discipline, who stood on either side of Hyegang, took the scissors and each made three cuts. Finally, another monk came with a straight razor and began shaving Hyegang's head in even strokes. In this way, Hyegang's head was completely shaved.

When Hyegang's head was clean, the other monks entered the main hall. They recited the *Heart Sutra* and the *Thousand Hands Sutra*, while offering sacrifices to the Buddha. After the recitation was completed, the Master of Truth, sitting on the seat of Truth and holding a bamboo staff, began speaking. He explained the essential truths of the universe. The Master of Discipline followed with an explanation of the ten rules that an apprentice monk must keep.

The rites concluded with the laying of a ceremonial robe and a wooden bell before Hyegang. The other monks helped him into his new robe. Because his name was one that was chosen by Monk Dasol when he was adopted, it could be used as his Buddhist name. Thus, Hyegang became Monk Hyegang.

I watched the proceedings with mixed emotions. Monk Dasol was a teacher for all people, a seeker of the Truth, one who pursues the attainment of the Buddhahood—this was clear to me now. His face shone like a star. It soothed the confusion in my mind.

After all the monks had left the hall, Monk Hyegang, still dressed in his ceremonial robe, came to me. I bowed with my hands clasped in front of me. "I pray that you become a great monk who will save all sentient beings."

His lips slightly pursed, Monk Hyegang bowed in return. "Thank you." The teacher-student relationship had become the relationship between a layperson and a monk.

Monk Dasol was watching us without expression. I remembered something he'd said once: "On a deeper level, you already knew him, through what we call oneness with Buddha."

After declining Monk Dasol's invitation to lunch at the temple, I walked back down the mountain road. My steps faltered many times.

Autumn had turned the sky a dazzling blue, and the leaves were vibrant in their colors. The weather was cool enough that we wore thick sweaters or coats. I was not sure if it was the changing of the season, but the pain in my chest was coming several times a day now. Sometimes, it was so intense, I wouldn't have been able to endure it without painkillers.

Doug came home around this time, worry on his face. "Mrs. Kang, you're still hurting."

"It seems to have gotten worse."

"I was worried about you. That's why I came," Doug said solemnly. "We'll go to the clinic tomorrow and get you in for a physical."

"Tomorrow is Sunday. The clinics are closed."

"Do you know any doctors?"

"An old friend of Jaun's father has an office in Jongno. He's an internist."

"We'll go there first. If he says there's no problem, it's all right. But if it's anything more serious than that, we can go to the clinic and see a specialist."

"That's a good idea." I appreciated his concern.

Chapter Ten: October

We went to Dr. Hong's office the next day. He recognized me immediately and welcomed us warmly. "Are you still teaching at the high school?"

"Yes."

"How is Jaun? She must be big now."

After a few everyday questions, he asked why I was there.

"I've been having this pain in my chest for several months now. I thought I should maybe get a check-up."

"Pain? Where?"

"Well, I don't know exactly. But it's been coming quite often."

Dr. Hong's face became serious, and he led me into the examination room. After some tests, he asked for me to return the next afternoon for the results. The expression on his face told me this was not a light matter.

I arrived home with confused thoughts moving about in my head. I missed my husband's care. I became aware how terrifying it is for a widow to fall sick.

"The results won't be in until tomorrow, so I'll go back to the farm and return tomorrow." Gloom cast a shadow over Doug's face.

"No. You don't have to. I know you have a lot of things to do. You can't just leave your work."

"I see life in a small plant or in a small flower, and I try to do my job as well as I can. But how can I think of anything else when you are sick?"

"You sound as if I'm on my deathbed already."

"I don't mean that. Anyway, I'll come back tomorrow."

After he left, I realized to my surprise that the boy I had looked after was now taking care of me. I was grateful for his consideration. At night, ideas of extreme possibilities crowded my mind while I tried to drive them away.

The pain came to me again in the morning. It rocked my body, and I shuddered at its stubbornness. By the time I arrived at the school, I was exhausted. This body that causes me so much pain—is it really mine?

"Mrs. Kang, you look so sick," the fine arts teacher said.

"I'm feeling a little sick."

"What's the matter?"

"My chest hurts."

I taught three classes and finished with closing session. It was a long and arduous day. I immersed myself in reading during recess, to forget the pain and to forget my worry. My reading these days consisted mostly of scriptures. I read the *Lotus Sutra*, the *Flower Garland Sutra*, the *Heart Sutra*, these in no particular order. I didn't try to understand what I read, but more read them as I would an assignment. It was like completing a promise I'd made to myself.

There was another attack of pain as I was about to leave the school. It was so severe that perspiration drenched my entire body. I took out the rosary from my purse.

"I hope you will cherish this for a long time. Whenever you find yourself in difficult times, you may call to the Bodhisattva the Compassionate." This is what Monk Dasol had said to me as he took this rosary from his neck and placed it around mine. That night, I'd wanted to cry, bury my head in his chest and cry like a child. My lonely soul—it had roamed all this time and now it wanted to put down roots. But his gray sacred robe was not the place for it. I knew too well it wasn't. There was despair and sorrow in this knowledge, but it also had beauty.

I now put the rosary in my lap and touched the beads one by one. "Gwanseeum Bosal, Gwanseeum Bosal."

Does she understand human yearning? Does she know the yearning that exists in our souls and in our bodies? If there is only emptiness, what gives forth to this yearning?

The beads made a full rotation around the tips of my fingers. I put the rosary back in my purse and left the staff room.

The fine arts teacher asked, "Should I go with you to the bus stop?"

"Do I look that bad?"

"No, I didn't mean that."

"Don't worry, I'm not that bad."

"Take care of yourself."

"I will."

I stopped in the schoolyard to watch some boys kick a soccer ball. I stayed awhile before leaving.

Wanting to delay my meeting with Dr. Hong, I walked past two bus stops before finally getting on a bus.

"It doesn't look serious," Dr. Hong said in his office. "But to be absolutely certain, I'd like for you to undergo an overall physical at the hospital."

"Do I have to?"

"Well, the equipment at these smaller clinics is not enough to be exactly certain."

"How long will it take?"

"You'll likely have to stay for about a week."

"That long?"

"Yes."

"Which hospital would you recommend?"

"Go to S. University Hospital. I'll write you a referral for Dr. Kim in the thoracic department. I want you to go see him."

I waited while Dr. Hong wrote out his letter of referral, then left the office with the it. As I made my way along the sidewalk outside, I toyed with the idea that it might be lung cancer. Then the idea became fact. I clenched my fists, telling myself to stop being silly.

It can't be. I'm not ready to die.

I entered a nearby teahouse and drank in my emotions over a cup of coffee. I needed somebody. I needed somebody who could chase away this desperate moment and reassure me everything was all right. I missed Monk Dasol. If only he were with me now. But he was so far away, far away where I couldn't touch him in my despair.

That great distance, in the thickness of his gray robe.

I finished my coffee and left the teahouse. After wandering around aimlessly for a while, I found myself in front of my house. Doug was there.

"What did the results say?"

"He recommended more tests."

"A full physical?" He looked at me for a moment. "Then you'd better get one. We'll go to the hospital tomorrow."

"What about my classes?"

"I'll go to your school and get you a sick leave."

"Wouldn't that look strange? I was fine today."

"There's nothing strange about it. Tomorrow morning, I'll go to the school and you get ready to go to the hospital," Doug said, his voice rising. It was an order.

"I think I need to prepare myself a little bit. I'll have to tell Jaun."

"The most difficult part will be explaining to Jaun, might as well be sooner than later. I'll arrange for her to stay at her aunt's for a while."

"Well."

"We need to handle this professionally. Just do as I say, please."

Doug didn't return to the farm that night. He probably knew that I was depending on him, which I was. I wondered if it was moments like these that made parents wish for sons.

I decided to listen to Doug. After a mostly sleepless night, I woke up to find Jaun in my room.

"Are you awake now?"

"Yes. I must have slept in."

"It's all right. You're not going to work."

"How did you know that?"

"Doug told me you were going away to the school's cottage."

"He told you that?"

"Yes."

I felt a piercing in my heart as Jaun stood there, smiling.

"I hope it's all right with you if I do that, Jaun," I said, trying to suppress my emotions.

"Of course. I'll stay at Aunt's while you're gone. You have a good rest."

Jaun didn't ask why I needed the rest. She believed what Doug told her. But Doug was right to say that it would be better for her to know soon.

Doug left for my school after breakfast and returned about two hours later, saying he'd submitted my application for sick leave.

We went to S. University Hospital and checked in, a complicated procedure. They took me to a room. There were so many patients, it seemed to me all the people in the world were patients. I changed into a hospital gown and lay down in the bed. Doug was in and out of my room, looking after the admission procedures.

This was the beginning of a long and boring stay at the hospital. I was taken to various places for tests, several times on some days. Sometimes, I wasn't sure if they were really trying to find out what was wrong or if they were conducting their own research.

During the stay, I ate when it was time to eat and slept when it was time to sleep. The goings on around the hospital reminded me of how precious a sound body was. I wanted so badly to be healthy again, to move and do things without thinking about it.

But health had turned its back on me. Now truly I possessed nothing in this world. Just as all things eventually return to their original place, my body was going back to where it had come from. What remained for me? My mind? But the mind is formless. Not only formless, but it is always changing, too vague to be identified with myself. So then the conclusion: the life I've lived is intangible, like a shadow.

Doug watched over me for the week I was at the hospital, without hesitation and without complaint. Waking from a confusing dream, I would find him at my bedside. Sometimes, I pretended to be sleeping, just to avoid looking into those eyes.

Finally, the last day of my stay had arrived. Time had a way of marching on through any situation.

"They'll let us know the results, won't they?" I asked.

"Sure they will."

"One day here seems like a thousand years."

"You've lived seven thousand years."

"You bet." Who knows that I haven't?

The doctor came after lunch, wanting to speak with Doug privately. The hair around his forehead was wet because he'd washed his face. I knew everything from looking into his bloodshot eyes. I had cancer.

"Did he tell you about the test results?" I asked when Doug came back into the room.

"Yes."

"What did he say?"

"He said it isn't serious."

"It's lung cancer, isn't it?"

"What?" Doug looked at me.

"Don't worry. I probably knew it when I came here."

Tears flooded Doug's eyes. "Mrs. Kang." He held my hand and began to sob as I stood looking down the edge of an imaginary cliff. My last hope, "possibly not," had betrayed me.

"How long did he say I had?" I asked, trying to stay composed.

"Three to six months."

"I see."

I could be gone in one hundred days. A hundred days was all the time I had in this world, all the time I had to bring closure. It might be enough.

"Can I leave the hospital now?"

"I'll go and arrange for your discharge."

"Good. And please phone my sister and ask her to have Jaun taken home."

"I will." Doug left the room while I tried not to think. There was only the hope that I could bring everything to a clean finish within the hundred days granted to me.

I had lived my life until now in preparation for this. It had been my aspiration to die with peace of mind. But now that the moment was near at hand, there seemed to be so many things to get done. It felt like I was returning without having done anything. I had been only a spectator in this world.

I got out of bed and changed into my clothes. After making the bed, I picked up the rosary, which I had hung on the headboard, and rolled the beads in my hand.

"Mrs. Kang, we can go now," Doug said.

"Shall we?" I stood up, and Doug followed me out with my things.

I had spent a long and boring time only to confirm my death. I left the hospital feeling a little cheated.

The sunshine streamed down on the streets outside. Its brilliance was almost too bright for my eyes. Cars swarmed, people moved past, buildings towered—they were of another world to me now, nothing to do with me. The world went on, taking no notice.

"Doug, would you mind getting these things home?"

"What about you?"

"There's somewhere I want to go right now. Could you go on ahead?"

"You can't go alone. If you want to go, I'll go with you."

"I'm not that sick yet. I'll be all right by myself," I insisted.

Doug considered for a while before finally agreeing. "Then take care of yourself. Be home soon."

After watching Doug leave, I took a taxi to Jeongreung. I needed to see Monk Dasol.

It was time to untie the attachment closest to my heart.

I got out of the taxi in front of Yeongdeung-sa Temple's main entrance and walked slowly up the mountain road. Brightly colored leaves fell. A distance up the road, I came to a spot from where I could see the roofs of the temple. I took a trail that led off the road and came to a small clearing. There I sat down on the fallen leaves on the ground. The trickle of the streams, the singing of the birds, the rustling of falling leaves—nature still breathed, maintaining things in their natural order.

Through the branches, I could see a narrow path that led to the temple. It was about six o'clock in the evening. Monk Dasol would probably be passing by soon. I lay down on the blanket of leaves, looking down on the path with the easy and wandering mind of a traveler. The birds flew about as they made their preparations for nightfall.

Then there was the gray robe of Monk Dasol. He walked slowly, seen from this view, a lonely figure.

Everybody is alone. People walk by themselves.

I watched his back, following him with my eyes as he walked away. Before long, he had disappeared.

As darkness crept through the mountains, I heard the sound of the evening bell at the temple.

I caught a bus for downtown and, after getting off at Jongno, went into the Bodhi Tree. The teahouse was quiet tonight. I took the table where I had sat with Monk Dasol. I remembered the sound of the forest breeze, the breeze I had heard at our first meeting. What did it mean to me?

The waitress glanced at me sideways as she set a cup of coffee on the table. I looked down at the brown coffee for a long time before taking a sip. As the warm coffee passed down my throat, it seemed to melt my body wherever it touched, leaving in its wake a deep sorrow that poured over me now. I closed my eyes and tried to swallow the sorrow.

How long had I been there? I opened my eyes and looked at the clock. It was nine o'clock. I paid the cashier and left the teahouse for the chilly night air. The wind blew against me, hard against my body. As I passed out of Anguk-dong and the government buildings toward Samcheong-dong, I heard my name being called from behind me. It was Doug.

"What are you doing out here?"

"Mrs. Kang, please, put this on." He took off his coat and draped it around my shoulders.

"Thank you, Doug."

He said nothing.

"Is Jaun sleeping?"

"She went to bed a little while ago."

"Doug, you can go back to the farm tomorrow morning."

"Well," he responded vaguely.

Sudden exhaustion swept over me as I arrived home. I went into Jaun's room. She was sleeping, her small body curled up under the covers. I knelt at her feet.

"This mother has to go, leave you on your own. The sinner."

I held Jaun's small feet tightly to my chest and wept out my sins.

CHAPTER ELEVEN:

December

The cold December rain fell, promising to leave cold weather in its wake. It always rains at the changing of seasons. From winter to spring, from spring to summer, from summer to autumn. Now I was not to see the arrival of another spring. Never again would I see the ocean in summer, a field in autumn. The absolute force of death was unstoppable. I could do nothing but accept it helplessly.

I decided that I would not go to the hospital again. I simply endured the pain or took painkillers. During very severe bouts, I could feel it to the tips of my fingers. But I would not go in for treatment. I refused to take this dying body back and forth, subjecting it to the care of people with their own agendas.

The thought of killing myself entered my mind many times, especially when the pain, already unbearable at times, seemed only to be getting worse. To the healthy, suicide is a moral issue; for a patient dying in pain, it is a form of deliverance.

Chapter Eleven: December

I looked forward to escaping the misery and finding rest. I continued to go to work, not just because it was a way to spend time but because there were things, important duties, I had to carry out in the time left to me.

I taught each class as best I could, giving close attention to the problems of each individual student. I welcomed each day as if it were my last, not to be repeated. The teachers and the students were aware my health was not good, but I didn't tell them I was dying.

My remaining days dwindled away one by one with the coming of each day and night. I'd spent November in this way. Now it was December. I prepared questions for winter exams and mimeographed a copy of the exam for each student in the class. I put the copies in an envelope and sealed it. On the front, I signed my name in red ink: Kihae Kang.

After looking at my name, I decided to erase it from the roll call. If I was to die before exams were over, it would be left there as a sad reminder to the teachers handing out these exams in my place. After locking the roll call and the exams in my desk drawer, I gave the key to the fine arts teacher. "I'm so forgetful these days. Could you hold onto this key for me?"

The fine arts teacher looked at me carefully but accepted the key without comment.

I stood up and walked into the chairman of the board's office with an envelope containing my letter of resignation and a small box containing a tie pin. Engraved onto the tie pin were the seven treasures.

"Thank you for everything," I said.

The chairman's eyes widened as he read over my letter. "Why are you doing this?" he asked.

"Health reasons. I'll work until the beginning of winter vacation."

"How bad is your health? Bad enough for you to have to quit?"

"Yes. I'm quite sick."

"You can take sick leave for the next semester. We'll hire a substitute."

"Thank you for your concern, but please accept my resignation. And this is just a small token of my appreciation. I hope you like it." I pushed the box toward him on the desk.

He looked at the box blankly and then, realizing that he wasn't going to dissuade me, finally took it. I said goodbye to the chairman and left his office. The teachers called him the Bear because of his stinginess and insensitivity, but I had a lot to thank him for. I had worked for more than ten years at his school. While closing the door to the office behind me, I silently wished him the best for the future.

Back in the staff room, I took out my students' report cards to fill out. On each card was pasted the photograph of a student, short-clipped hair and black uniform. As I looked into these faces one by one, I wrote down my remarks, trying to be as positive as possible. This was my final encouragement and advice to them. As I went through the cards one by one, I said a silent goodbye to each.

Chapter Eleven: December

With the official matters at the school almost completed, there was the final problem of Jaun. This child who had come into the world through my body, this lonely child who missed her father—I had to bring hurt to this child. How horrible it was. The most horrible thing in the world, a sin. How had the actions of a sinner been assigned to me? Was it karma accumulated from previous lives? Then when will I find redemption for this sin I'm about to commit in this life?

"Mrs. Kang." Hyegang stood before me, his shaven head contrasting sharply with his black uniform. "Could I talk with you in the counseling room?"

"What is it, Hyegang?"

Hyegang didn't answer, but just stared at me, his face white and waxen. I stood up and went to the counseling room with him.

"Take a seat there." I indicated a chair and took a place myself on the sofa.

He sat silently in front of me before he spoke. "Mrs. Kang, why didn't you tell me?" Tears ran down his cheeks.

I had nothing to say.

"Why didn't you tell me?" he said again. I felt the cutting in my heart. This boy, who needed my help—to him, too, I had to say goodbye. A dreadful silence took over the room. Separation is such a difficult task. What is attachment? What is affection? What are these things?

"Hyegang, you're a monk. You should rid yourself of all personal attachments and be a great monk. Isn't this right?"

"I need you, Mrs. Kang. You should be there to watch me grow and become a great monk. I need you watching me."

"I wish I could. But it's not up to me, is it?"

Hyegang didn't answer.

"How did you find out?" I asked.

"I went to see Doug yesterday. He told me everything. Then I went to the university hospital, hoping it was a mistake."

"Why did you do that?"

Again, he didn't answer.

"I'm trying my best to hold onto the end like this. As a monk, you should be encouraging me."

"You will always be my teacher."

"I appreciate that. That's why I don't treat you the same as other monks," I said. "By the way, have you finished your statue of the Bodhisattva the Compassionate?"

"No. I will never finish it."

"I've wanted to see the Bodhisattva the Compassionate, as you envision her."

"You can go home now," I said when he said nothing. "I believe we will have time to visit again."

As he left the room, Hyegang looked back with his pale face to me once more before turning away, his lips quivering. I sunk back into the sofa. Cold air drifted up from the cement floor.

The last time I was in this room was with Soktae, when life's beginning was a sin. Today, life's end was a sin.

I recalled the faces of people I had met in my lifetime. There were ones I was happy to remember; some I wasn't.

I thought I should go and see the people I was thankful to have met. In a sense, my gratitude was a debt I owed them, and I would feel better repaying that debt. But then the faces of people I disliked rose from memory. My mind, in the face of impending death, had become generous enough to remember them.

As I returned to the staff room, the fine arts teacher looked up. Apparently finding something wrong, he said, "Mrs. Kang, you don't look well."

"It was cold in the counseling room. Maybe that's why."

"You could use a vacation. Why don't you take one?" he said in a sympathetic tone.

"I'll be resting peacefully soon."

The fine arts teacher blinked, trying to make meaning of what I'd said.

The man deserved my gratitude. He was a little crude at times but always open-minded. And his presence in the school had made my stay much more entertaining.

"Is there anything you want?" I asked the fine arts teacher.

"What?"

"I'd like to get you a Christmas gift."

"Well, what should I ask for?"

"Anything."

"Anything? What is that?" He cocked his head upwards. "When you say that, I can't think of anything. I guess what you would like. So, what should I get you?"

"Who would demand a gift?" I said, and we laughed.

Jaun was waiting at the bus stop as I arrived. "Were you all right today, Mom?"

"I was fine."

"You didn't have the pain today?"

"Not even once."

"That's great. You must be getting better."

"Yes, I think so."

Jaun took my purse and linked her free arm around mine.

"Jaun, how would you like a new woolen cap?"

"The one I have now is still good."

"Yes. That's pretty, too. But I want to see what you'll look like when you go to middle school next year."

Jaun was quiet but wasn't suspicious. I took her hand and put it in my coat pocket. Poor girl, who will attend your middle school graduation? Emotion tightened my throat, and I had to turn my head away.

"Mom, Aunt is waiting at our house for you. She came about an hour ago."

"Is Donghoon with her?"

"No, she came by herself."

My sister was the one to answer the gate when I rang the bell.

"Kihae, can't you please stop going to work?"

"Why should I stop if I can still go?"

"Good heavens, what's the matter with you, Kihae?" My sister shot me a dirty look.

"Let's go in. It's cold."

"Auntie, will you turn on the stove? Okay?" my sister called into the house. "You should stop being so cheap. Why do you leave the house so cold?"

"It's an old house. There's no central heating."

"You should have got one installed a long time ago."

"We don't need to change seasons in the house like you do in yours. I've lived this long without too much trouble."

"There you go again. No wonder you ended up like—" She stopped herself from finishing the sentence.

The fire was burning blue in the kerosene stove when we walked into my room. I lay down in bed and asked if Jaun could go to the store with Dougienei. She looked at me and then my sister. "All right," she replied.

Pain shook through me after Jaun had left the room. I closed my eyes and braced against it.

"Kihae, what can I do?" my sister said tearfully, holding my arm to her chest. "Kihae, I was thinking. We can talk to Donghoon's father and see about getting you treated in the United States. How about that?"

The pain, after mincing through every cell in my body it seemed, slowly began to subside. The devil was at play.

"Is your husband in the United States now?"

"Yes. How about it, Kihae?"

"What if I die there?"

"Don't talk about death. You'd be going there to be cured."

"Don't be silly. I don't want to die like that."

"Think about living. How come you're trying to die?"

"It gives me comfort, to accept it as a natural passage."

"Why do you keep sounding like Confucius?" my sister screamed, angry at my lukewarm attitude.

Sounding like Confucius? I wondered if even Confucius had accepted his death undisturbed.

"I'm going to owe you everything. Please take good care of Jaun."

My sister sobbed into my arm.

"Don't be like this. I'm dying," I said evenly.

My sister began sobbing more bitterly at this. "Poor you." I wanted to cry with her, cry with abandon. But I had no one to cry for. Maybe that was what my sister was referring to.

"Let's finish our talk before Jaun comes back. After I'm gone, sell the house and save half of the money in a trust for Jaun and use the other half to raise her."

"Kihae, how is it possible? How can a nice and intelligent person like you live only for such a short time and die?" My sister was still crying.

I turned over in my bed.

"I'm sorry, Kihae. I'm so helpless to be burdening you with sorrow like this." She left the room, wanting to wash her face before Jaun returned.

I heard Doug's voice outside. It must be evening, for him to have returned now. One of the reasons why I kept my job was so that Doug would keep going to work. When it became clear that I was keeping my job, he stopped talking about quitting his. But he came home every evening to check up on me.

As painful as it is to feel attachment or affection—and even if they are the cause of delusions and illusions—they are to me the most beautiful things in the world. They are what helps me survive in this world. Without this final opportunity to confirm my warm affection to those who loved me, my way toward the last would have been much lonelier.

The last day of school before winter vacation was gray and dull. I cleaned my desk and packed my things. I said goodbye to the students. In the staff room, the other teachers threw me a farewell party. It was amusing to wonder if there would be one when I left this world, but otherwise, these things held little meaning for me. The last moments of my life now made up only a brief span of sunlight, and I didn't want to waste even one on useless things like a party.

The board chairman paid me my retirement fund, pension, and bonus in addition to the last month's salary. I added this money to the money I had brought from home and deposited it all into a savings account opened under Monk Dasol's name. I wrote a short letter: "This is some money I could not use. Please allow me to entrust it in your care, to be used at your discretion." I put the letter, the passbook, and the seal into an envelope and mailed the package to Yeongdeung-sa Temple.

I dropped in at a clothing store and bought a thick sweater and a wool underskirt for the old woman in Cheongsol before going to Seoul Station to meet Monk Dasol.

This trip to Cheongsol would be my final farewell to Monk Dasol. I wanted to say goodbye before deterioration set in.

I arrived at the station to find Monk Dasol waiting for me as before. His face was dark with despair. He knows everything. He knows I am dying. He knows this is our last day. I could read this on his face.

Monk Dasol walked over to where I was. "You must be cold," he said tenderly, as if speaking to a child.

"I am."

"Do you think you'll be able to go?"

"I want to."

"I've bought two tickets." There were two tickets in his hand, each with the name Cheongsol written on them. Before, at seeing these tickets, I saw the fate of two people going to the same place. Was it still to be?

Monk Dasol and I barely spoke until our arrival in Cheongsol. Empty fields spread out before us. The dark green rice stalks, the storks flying overhead, the golden waves—they had all disappeared, like a mirage.

"It looks like it's going to snow," I said, looking up at the sky.

"It does."

We fell silent again and continued walking through the empty field.

"It's not Sunday today. Most of the people may be at work," I said.

Monk Dasol didn't respond.

"That bridge looks longer. Maybe because it's winter," I said, pointing.

Chapter Eleven: December

"Maybe because it's lonely."

I glanced at his face. What a curious remark. The sky hung low on the horizon and birds floated over the river.

We crossed the bridge into the hamlet. The huts that looked like stables lay still, like death in the immense stillness. Children were playing with a skipping rope, but they scattered when they saw us.

"Shall we visit the old woman?" I suggested.

Monk Dasol nodded without saying anything.

We stepped into the hut. Chilly air filled the room even inside, and lying in the middle was the old woman, curled up like a pupa. The sight of her bent body seized me with sympathy. This woman does not receive even the blessing of a short piece of thread. If I could live longer, I would come from time to time just to change her clothes.

"Grandmother, how have you been?"

The old woman, sensing a presence, got up slowly. I dressed her in the thick sweater I'd brought. There was no longer the disgust or nausea, as before. I buttoned the front to the top and arranged it neatly before beginning with her wool underskirt. After, I squeezed some Won bills into her hand.

The old woman rubbed her shoulder with one hand as she looked at the money. I put my own hand on her shoulder and said, "Goodbye, and take care of yourself."

Monk Dasol had been watching me silently. I quickly turned away when my eyes met his and left the hut.

A woman was coming out of another hut. "Good heavens," the woman exclaimed loudly. "Oh, Master, how good to see you!"

We were happy to see her face again. It had been her plea to Monk Dasol that first day that had begun our special relationship with this village.

"Why are you at home today?" Monk Dasol asked.

"I peddle all over the place, and I rest when I want."

"I see."

"Master, would you come into my hut?"

Monk Dasol looked at me.

"Shall we?" I said, and we stepped inside.

The hut was small but clean and neatly arranged. There was a radio, and in a vase on it, there were some artificial flowers.

"This is a nice room," Monk Dasol said.

"Before I became like this, I was quite well off."

"I see."

"But it's useless to talk about the past now. It's like walking around at night wearing silk."

"Did you attend a Buddhist temple?"

"I used to run a yardage shop, and during that time, I went quite regularly. I donated to the temple often, too."

"I see."

"But Buddha has no pity. How could he let leprosy into my body?" She sighed.

"One can suffer for karma accumulated in previous lives. But if you live righteously in this life, you may be blessed and live comfortably in your next," Monk Dasol said, smiling.

"Master, please, wait just a few minutes. I'll steam some sweet potatoes for you. It won't take long." She went into the kitchen without giving us a chance to refuse. We sat against the wall as she clanged pots and pans.

While we were waiting for the sweet potatoes, a stabbing pain shot through my body. I bit my lip, my body in perspiration. Monk Dasol took out his handkerchief and wiped away the beads of sweat on my face. Through my pain, I wanted to throw myself into his arms and cry. But again, I fought the impulse.

The woman came out with a basket of potatoes. It belched thick white steam. "Master, please have some. Bosal-nim, please."

"Thank you."

"Gracious heavens. Look at it outside. It's snowing so much. It must be ankle-deep already."

"Is it really?" I asked, politely.

"I wonder why the first snowfall of the season is always so heavy." With deformed hands, she peeled a sweet potato and held it out to Monk Dasol. He accepted it and ate it in silence. I too peeled one and ate it. After finishing, I stood up. "Should we leave now?"

"Yes. We'd better go."

"Have just one more."

"Thank you, but I'm not feeling well."

"Bosal-nim, you used to be so beautiful, like an angel. Why is your face like this now? I wanted to ask you before."

"I've been sick."

"What is it?"

"Goodbye."

"Goodbye. But, Master, you will come again, won't you?"

"I will."

We turned to go. As the woman had said, it was snowing hard outside. The snow on the ground was already up to our ankles. The snow on the pine trees looked like white cranes.

When we reached the bridge, Monk Dasol noticed that I was shivering and took the thick scarf from his shoulders to wrap around me. Then he asked me to wait a moment while he walked back in the direction of the village.

I watched the snowflakes falling into the river, one by one. In the scene, I thought I could see the standing figure of Monk Dasol reciting the scriptures, his hand striking a wooden bell. I closed my eyes and the scene disappeared.

Monk Dasol returned after a few minutes, a pine branch in his hand. With it, he began sweeping away the snow that had accumulated on the bridge. Even as he swept, fresh snow alighted on the bridge, forming a thin haze. After sweeping clear to the other side, he walked back to me and, taking firm hold of my hand, asked me to cross with him.

"Yes."

My hand in Monk Dasol's, we started across the bridge. The warmth of his hand cast sadness through me. When we had reached the other side, he opened his arms and embraced me tightly. In his arms, I became a woman. Warm tears ran between our faces.

The empty fields were white—heaven and earth ecstatic in their whiteness. It was a new world, inhabited only by Monk Dasol and me. The snow continued to fall while we walked under the blessings of the heavens and the blessings of our new world.

Sudden pain swept up my body. Terrifying and unrelenting, it gave no indication of ever ceasing.

"Monk Dasol, it hurts too much." I pressed my face into his chest.

"Let's rest in there." His arms around my shoulders, Monk Dasol led me to a deserted hut that sat on the river bank. "Will you wait here a moment?"

Leaving me at the door, he went into the kitchen and came out a few moments later with old scraps of paper. He arranged the paper in the wood stove with some broken lengths of board. He took out a box of matches and lit one. He held the match to the paper until it began to burn. The fire started, he looked around the room and, after finding an old broom, swept it clean.

Smoke began to fill the room. It went outside through the torn-out paper in the door like clouds and disappeared.

"Shall we go in?" Monk Dasol gently brushed the snow from my head and my shoulders.

The room began to warm. Monk Dasol took off his outer robe and spread it across the doorway to keep the snow out. He carried an old hardwood door into the room and, after laying it on the floor, spread my overcoat atop it. He helped me to lie down on the coat and lay down beside me.

White snowflakes floated in through the broken windows.

"Monk Dasol, I wonder what law of causation brought us together."

"That of petals." He opened his arms and held me tightly. I cried into his chest.

Petals. Was our relationship the relationship between flower petals? Would we ever meet again? Somewhere beyond the heavens?

I closed my eyes. The thirty-six years I had lived went by in a mere moment. Kalpas endless time floated; kalpas endless time.

White snowflakes tumbled from the sky. The flakes turned into azalea petals. Pink ones, they shouted as they lighted into the room. One, then two, ten, one thousand, ten thousand... the petals were now dancing waves. We were among them now. Peace took us in its embrace. It was a moment of eternity.

EPILOGUE:
The Ritual of Cremation

Monk Hyegang has finished reading my mother's journal.

"It's a beautiful story," I say to Monk Hyegang. "I wonder what happened after that? The journal ends in winter, but it wasn't until March twenty-sixth that she passed away."

"They stopped meeting after that."

"Then, Master Dasol didn't know about Mother's death?"

"That morning in March, I was called to Master Dasol's room. When I went there, he was burning incense and copying down the *Diamond Sutra*."

"The *Diamond Sutra*?"

"Yes. While he was copying this down, his face—how can I say it? I remember that expression, but I can find no words to describe it even now."

"What happened then?"

"After he finished copying the sutra, he gave the copy to me and said, 'Take this to your teacher's house.' I ran with it as fast as I could, but when I got to your house, I could hear people crying."

I wait for Monk Hyegang to continue.

"Your mother had passed away just as I got there."

"I see."

"I went inside and her body was there. She was holding a rosary in her hands, across her chest, and her face was so beautiful. Maybe it was because she was no longer suffering. She looked at peace. How can I say it? She looked like an angel? Immortal? She looked like a woman who had transcended.

"I took the *Diamond Sutra* Master Dasol had copied and spread it over her body. And I recited the sutra. At that moment, the Bodhisattva the Compassionate appeared to me. The Bodhisattva, whom I had tried so hard to visualize all this time—she appeared before me!"

"The Bodhisattva the Compassionate?"

"Yes. I had to mold that image right away. So I ran to the school and, after locking myself in the fine arts room, began working. After I finished, I came out with the statue in my arms. It was dark outside by then.

"I went back to your house with the statue, and a folding screen had been placed in front of your mother's body. I put down the statue in front of the screen. You bowed to it and cried, 'Hyegang, when did you mold my mother's image?' The statue of the Bodhisattva the Compassionate had your mother's face!"

"It must have been because you loved my mother so much."

"Three days later, after the funeral service, I went back to the temple to find that Master Dasol had gone to Hongryun-am to pray. Without even stopping in at my room, I went there. When I got to the temple, they told me he had been fasting for three days without ever coming out of the prayer hall."

"Is that right?"

Monk Hyegang places a few blocks of wood into the fire. "Aren't you cold?" he asks.

"No, I'm all right."

Monk Hyegang gazes at the ashes of Master Dasol's body. "Master Dasol gave me a passbook the day before he died. He said, 'This is what your teacher left in my care. There's her money and some of what I saved. You keep it and put it to good use. I've been visiting Cheongsol twice a month. They probably think I'm from a nearby temple. If you want, you should visit there someday.'"

"So, Master Dasol continued to visit Cheongsol even after my mother had died."

"Yes. I didn't know that either."

We sit in silence for a while. Slim lines of white smoke rise from the ashes. The heart of that master suffered from human attachment.

"I'd like to go with you when you visit Cheongsol."

"You would?"

"Yes, I would."

Monk Hyegang doesn't say anything. The heavy silence again comes over us.

"Why didn't you pursue your art?"

"When your mother was dying, I felt so helpless. Even now when I'm working at the hospital, I wonder from time to time which room your mother stayed in when she was there."

"What should we do with this journal?" I ask.

"Well, what should we do?"

"I think we should give it to Master Dasol."

Monk Hyegang looks at me. "I believe that would be a good idea," he agrees.

Monk Hyegang and I stand and clasp our hands before us as we look into the fire. We throw the journal, the account of his and my mother's life together. The journal dissolves into flames and rises with the body of the master. In the distance, dawn breaks along the mountain ridges.